THE CORPSE AT RAVENHOLM CASTLE

LADY THEA'S MYSTERY: BOOK 2

JESSICA BAKER

Book Two of the *Lady Thea's Mysteries Series*

First edition: August 2020

ISBN: (paperback) 978-1-7347202-3-5
ISBN: (e-book) 978-1-7347202-2-8

Published 2020 by Jessica Cobine

ACKNOWLEDGMENTS

Thank you to:

My parents who support and believe in me.

Shanté, my writing partner,
without whom I would have lost my mind.

Jerri for all of your help and support.

Everyone who has been supportive of me
since I've started this journey.

And all that read *Murder on the Flying Scotsman.*

DISCLAIMER

While it is possible to read this book first, for the most enjoyable reading experience, please read Book 1, Murder on the Flying Scotsman, before reading this one.

CHAPTER ONE

1910, SCOTLAND

Of all the places in Great Britain she had traveled, Lady Theodora Prescott-Pryce thought her cousins' home, Ravenholm Castle in Scotland, was the prettiest.

During this visit, Thea had explored every one of the seventy rooms in depth. She found the only two rumored secret passages in the castle, though her cousins, Anthony and Charlotte McNeil, believed there had to be more. Thea didn't think so, considering she had combed through every square inch of the castle. She had moved every book on the shelves in the library, tugged on every sconce, and tapped on every wooden panel. Nothing had moved and there were no odd drafts that suggested that there was something else hidden behind them.

Simply put, Thea was bored.

After all the excitement on her train journey from London on the *Flying Scotsman*, sitting all day—socializing and being a proper lady—didn't hold the same thrill as solving a murder.

She hadn't heard from Molly at all since she'd been there. Thea had written multiple letters to her former maid but they had all gone unanswered. She wished she knew what was going on with her. Being a widow running a successful department store on her own couldn't be easy. Trying to set those affairs in order with a baby on the way had to be incredibly difficult. She had no idea how Molly was managing it so soon after her husband's murder.

Daniel Talbot, Molly's husband and one of the co-founders of the department store Fletcher's, was murdered on the train. Molly had been framed for his murder.

A knock on the door startled her from her musings. Thea turned to see her cousin Lady Charlotte—Charlie—standing in the hallway.

"Are you doing anything today?"

Thea shook her head. "No. Why?"

"It's a nice day. I was thinking of taking a walk around the grounds. Would you care to join me?"

Thea set her pen down. Molly didn't need another letter from her. She'd let her know if she needed help. Thea just didn't want her to feel like she was alone.

"That would be nice."

THE WEATHER WAS PLEASANT. SINCE SHE ARRIVED, IT STORMED the first three days and the following two days were gloomy and threatened rain. It was strange to experience so much rain during one of her visits. But the sun had finally come out and it looked like it was going to be a beautiful day.

They walked outside along the path. The gardens at Ravenholm weren't as elaborate or flowery as her brother's Yorkshire manor. There were no winding paths and no ponds dotting the grounds.

The whole castle was walled off, protected by ivy-covered stone towers. The loch spread across the southern half of the grounds towards the village.

In some of her previous trips up there, Thea and her

cousins had taken the boat across the lake to spend the day strolling around the town. She always loved the smell of the freshly made shortbread sold at the little tearoom off of the apothecary. It made for a peaceful day.

But the gardens at Ravenholm—despite being lacking compared to her family's manor Astermore's sprawling hedges —were still Thea's favorite part of the grounds.

Charlie kept shooting her glances. Thea didn't want to say anything, didn't want to ask her cousin why she kept looking at her so strangely.

She lost that battle quickly. "What's wrong?"

Charlie shook her head. "I'm just worried about you. You've been quiet ever since what happened on the train."

Thea nodded.

"I read an article by your Mr. Poyntz this morning," Charlie said suddenly, as if she thought the change in subject might make Thea more talkative.

"He's not my Mr. Poyntz."

Thea met journalist James Poyntz on the train. There was something strange about him that she hadn't been able to put her finger on. She felt like she knew him but couldn't quite place from where. He had saved her life from the murderer and asked for nothing in return.

"What was the article about?" Thea asked her cousin.

"It's a fascinating series. He's been following around this man who built a monoplane. Baird, I think the fellow's name is."

Charlie shrugged. It would have been easy to be fooled by her reaction, but Charlie had been completely enthralled by the idea of flying. She even had a subscription to *Flight Magazine*, after discovering drawings of the Wright Brothers' powered aircraft in Anthony's copy of *The Automotor Journal*.

"Have you heard anything from Mr. Poyntz?" Charlie asked.

Thea shook her head. "Not since he sent that note with the article about the murder on the *Flying Scotsman*."

However, she had heard from Detective Inspector Leslie Thayne, whom she also met on the train. They exchanged several letters since arriving in Scotland. Inspector Thayne even sent her a telegram with news about the investigation from the events on the *Flying Scotsman*.

"Have you written to Mr. Poyntz?" Charlie's question caught her off-guard. Her thoughts had wandered to the inspector.

Thea glared at her cousin.

"You should," Charlie continued without paying attention to Thea's response, eyes wide at the prospect of speaking to him, "I'd love to get a chance to talk to him about his stories."

"I'll write to him," she promised, before she took a turn towards the large stone tower that she'd enjoyed climbing in past visits. Being in the tower made her feel like she had stepped into an adventure from one of her books.

The East Tower was nothing more than a folly, purposely built to look like the ruins of a medieval castle. It had been built sometime in the seventeen hundreds, though three different earls claimed responsibility for the creation of the tower. Since it overlooked the loch that belonged to them, it served no practical purpose other than to be decorative. She wasn't entirely sure how crumbling ruins were a fashionable look but it wasn't like Astermore didn't have its own folly, though their tower had been built fully intact.

"No!" Charlie shouted, grabbing her arm and yanking her back like she was a child wandering too close to a fire. Thea turned to stare at her. "It's haunted."

"You don't really believe that, do you?" Thea asked her cousin, watching the other girl eye the walls like someone might be hiding, ready to jump out.

"Of course, I do!" Charlie cried, pulling her jacket around

her tighter and shivering, despite the heat. She turned and marched back toward the castle.

"Why?" Thea asked as she followed her. "It wasn't when we were children."

Charlie shook her head. Her eyes were wide, filled with terror. She'd never known Charlie to be so afraid about anything. "Something happened a few years ago at the hunt. It was the year you didn't come up here, because of your father."

Thea pressed her lips together and glanced away. That was six years ago. That year, her father died suddenly and her family didn't make the trip to Ravenholm.

"Some of us were in the garden to look at the night sky and we thought we heard what sounded like a terrible scream from that direction. We looked, but no one could find anything." Charlie's knuckles were nearly white where they clenched at her jacket. "Some of the servants said they heard something out there, like a woman begging." She shuddered.

"Do you think something happened?" Thea asked, unable to help glancing over her shoulder. "Was someone killed?"

Charlie pressed her lips together until they lost their color. She shook her head. "I don't know. No one ever goes in there anymore."

"Why is this the first I'm hearing about this?"

"Because no one wanted to talk about it. It was easier to pretend nothing ever happened and avoid the tower." Charlie laughed bitterly.

Thea paused, looking back as she let Charlie continue on without her.

CHAPTER TWO

Promising to write to Mr. Poyntz was one thing. Actually sitting down and writing to him was another.

It was the next day before Thea put pen to paper. She had procured one of the morning newspapers and flipped through until she found one of Mr. Poyntz's articles. A small picture of a one-winged plane, called a monoplane, accompanied the story. The plane looked mostly like a skeleton of a creature and the idea something like that could stay in the air was bizarre. It reminded her of the contraption that crossed the English Channel the year before. She saw one in-person last year when she stopped in at Selfridges. Despite the fact she knew next to nothing about flying machines, she thought the article was rather good.

Dear Mr. Poyntz, she started, before pausing. What exactly could she say to him?

> *I trust all is well.*
> *My cousin, Lady Charlotte, has been reading your articles about Andrew Blain Baird's monoplane. She would like to meet you and discuss them. Please let me know at your earliest convenience.*

Sincerely,
Lady Theodora Prescott-Pryce

She stared at the words on the page. She really wasn't sure what else she could write to him. What did you say to someone who had appeared like some sort of avenging angel, welding a revolver and rescuing her from the murderer on a moving train? Someone who had practically disappeared from her life as quickly as he had appeared?

She set the pen down and sighed, folding the paper with careful creases. She addressed the envelope to James Poyntz at the *West End Gazette* headquarters in London and hoped they would forward it on to him in Scotland. She wondered where he was staying.

She gave it to Mr. Semple, the butler, to post and hoped for the best.

WANDERING THE GARDENS DID NOT KEEP HER MIND FROM THE letter, wondering how Mr. Poyntz would respond, if he even would respond. What if he didn't get the letter until he was back in London? Charlie would be disappointed but there wasn't much she could do about it.

Before she knew it, the East Tower loomed over her. This time, there was no Charlie to stop her.

She glanced back towards the castle. No one would notice she was gone until dinnertime. Thea had never believed in ghosts. She and her cousins played in the tower as children and she had never so much as seen a strange light or heard an unexplainable sound coming from there. But if there really was a ghost, she wanted to see it.

She tugged on the handle. The door hinges were rusty

from years of disuse and when the door finally opened, it let out a low groan.

Everything was mustier than Thea remembered it being. The floor was coated in a thick layer of grime and dust. The mold hung heavily in the air, so dense she could barely breathe without choking.

It was ridiculous to think that the tower was suddenly haunted and no one was coming in to clean or play anymore. Still, it couldn't hurt to have a look around. Maybe there was something to explain what they had heard six years ago.

The ground floor was mostly intact, but it appeared the ceiling now leaked.

She and her cousins used to bring blankets to the top floor and stare up at the stars. From the way Charlie had reacted to being outside the tower, she doubted they ever would do such a thing again.

She jumped as she heard something that sounded like a dying bird.

"Hello?"

Thea shook her head. She felt silly for calling out as if she expected someone to answer.

But then the noise came again. Softer. Scared.

She walked forward, hoping she wasn't making a mistake.

A furry ear popped up behind a pile of rubble. Then another. She nearly jumped back as one of the tiniest kittens she had ever seen lifted its head and let out another cry.

She never particularly liked cats, not after her grandmother's cat had sunk its teeth into the soft skin of her hand, between her forefinger and thumb. She still had the scars. The cat hadn't been scolded that day but her grandmother had boxed Thea's ears for upsetting poor dear Arnold.

She didn't have anything against them in general. They were useful for keeping pests away, especially around her family's manor where rodents often tormented the peacocks. Thea was just more comfortable when cats weren't around her.

But this one looked so sad and scared with its tiny body and head too big for its shoulders that she couldn't help but stare.

"Stop looking at me like that," she ordered as it blinked its big greenish-blue eyes up at her.

"Mrow?"

Thea frowned and pulled off her jacket and laid it on the ground. Tentatively, as if the kitten was afraid Thea might strike, it took a step forward. Then another. Another, until its whole body lay curled up in the middle. The kitten probably would have fit in the jacket pocket.

She sighed, kneeling down to pick up the bundle. The tiny creature shook in her hands, the tremors so hard that she could feel it through the jacket.

"Careful," she warned the creature as it squirmed. She didn't want to drop it but she probably would if it kept moving like that. Was there a way you were supposed to hold a cat? Was it like a baby?

Why was it here? The kitten didn't look old enough to be without its mother and Thea doubted it had been there for six years.

"Mrrrooow!" it wailed, its tiny fangs on display.

"I guess you're hungry."

What did cats eat? Mice, obviously but kittens couldn't do that. Or could they? Maybe someone in the kitchen would know.

"I'm going to look upstairs," she told it… him? Her? How did one tell if a cat was a boy or a girl? She almost unwrapped the jacket but imagined that the cat might scratch her. How old did kittens have to be before they had claws and could scratch?

Thea shook her head.

"I'll get you some food when we go back to the castle."

The kitten stared up at her, eyes wide, almost like it understood. Maybe it did.

CHAPTER THREE

When Thea reached the first floor, a sense of dread overwhelmed her. Something was not right. She could feel it in her very bones.

It didn't help that the kitten kept making these pitiful little whimpering noises, like it too could feel they shouldn't be there. Perhaps that's what Charlie meant by the tower suddenly being haunted.

The room looked as barren as the last time she was in there, but now, the roof had collapsed. Water pooled in the corner in the fireplace but seemed to drain into the back wall. That fireplace had been purposely functional so that people could still enjoy the tower in the winter months.

Thea stepped forward to get a better look. Most of the damage seemed centered around that area.

She leaned down and looked into the fireplace. For a second, Thea thought she saw something catch the light. She prodded at the wall. The stone was loose but not enough to budge.

The kitten let out a wail, and she jumped.

"What is it?" she asked softly, as if the creature could actually answer.

It stared up at her, large eyes fearful. It knew something wasn't right as much as she did.

She wrapped the jacket tighter around the kitten so it couldn't escape before setting the whole bundle down on the floor. The kitten mewled loudly, apparently upset with being put down.

"I know," Thea muttered. She tugged slightly at the stone again. A once white piece of fabric fluttered where it was trapped between the stones, frayed lace sticking out along the edges. A bit of black was caught with it. It looked oddly like one of the maid's dresses. Thea jumped back.

"We need to get some help in here." She felt slightly less ridiculous talking to the kitten and pretending it could understand her. She leaned down and picked up the kitten. "I think there's something in there. Let's go get some help."

"Meow."

She held the kitten close as she made her way to the castle as fast as she could. Realistically she knew that whatever was behind that wall was not going anywhere but she didn't want to take a chance.

Anthony happened to be passing by as Thea raced back.

"What happened?" Anthony asked.

"I was exploring in the East Tower," Thea told him and watched as his face paled.

"But it's haunted."

"So Charlie said," Thea muttered under her breath. "I think I found something in one of the fireplaces on the first floor."

Anthony stared at her for a long moment before he nodded. "I'll go find Father and then you can show us what you found." He glanced down at the kitten in her arms. "Where did you find that?"

"It was in the tower." She held the bundle out to him, and Anthony took it.

"And where is its mother?"

Thea shook her head. "I have no idea."

He nodded and together they walked to the drawing room. Anthony set the kitten onto one of the couches and moved to pull the cord in the corner of the room, signaling for one of the staff to come. He turned back to her. "I'm going to go find Father."

Thea nodded and took a seat at the other end of the couch. It was only a moment before a maid in a black dress and white lacy apron appeared in the room.

"Please take this kitten for something to eat," Thea told the maid. *Maybe someone can find it a home.*

The maid bowed her head, reached out to take the kitten, and disappeared out the door with the bundle in her arms. It was about at that moment that Anthony came back, his father walking beside him. The two of them were whispering softly but quieted abruptly when they entered the room.

"Please don't stop on my account," she said.

"Anthony was just telling me that you think you found something in the East Tower," her uncle said, though it sounded more like a question.

Anyone looking at Anthony and Malcolm McNeil could clearly see that Anthony got his good looks from his father. They wore similarly cut suits. It was almost unfair that both men could be so handsome.

"It looks like part of a maid's uniform and it was stuck in the fireplace. It looked like dried blood nearby too."

Uncle Malcolm glanced at his son and Thea wished she knew what he was thinking.

"Will you be all right to show us where?" he asked. She nodded.

The walk through the gardens and the grounds that afternoon hadn't seemed nearly as foreboding as it did this time. Even with Anthony and Uncle Malcolm by her side, she nearly turned back.

Thea swallowed as they got to the tower. Uncle Malcolm reached for the door and pulled it open.

"Where was it you saw this?" he asked.

"Upstairs."

She led the two men up the stairs and over to the fireplace where she had seen the material.

"There," Thea told them, pointing to the back wall.

Her uncle ducked his head into the fireplace.

"There's a lever high up!" he called a moment later. He pulled and part of the back popped. Uncle Malcolm stepped out and he and Anthony pulled the door open. A small recess was revealed along with the remains of a person.

Bits of a bloodied lace cap and auburn hair covered most of the object's skull.

"There's someone back here," Malcolm said.

She swallowed.

She had prepared herself mentally for seeing someone trapped behind the wall. Knowing was one thing. Actually seeing the corpse, really more of a skeleton clothed in the same black dress that the rest of the maids wore, was another.

"I'll call the police," Anthony said softly.

He darted down the stairs as quickly as he could without being called a coward.

Her uncle swallowed as he turned away from the fireplace. He shook his head. "We should move downstairs. Or would you prefer to go back to the main house?"

Thea gave him a shaky half-smile. "I'm all right."

In reality, she was wondering how fast she could make it to

the post office in the village. She wanted to send a telegram to Inspector Thayne. She trusted him to handle this matter with care. Her promise to him about leaving the crime-solving to the professionals was still fresh in her mind.

Uncle Malcolm stared at her and guided her down the stairs anyway. She must have looked worse than she felt, since he didn't let go of her until they were safely on the ground floor.

"It might be best for you to go to the house," he tried again, "This is a rather delicate matter."

Thea pressed her lips together.

"I know. But I'm the one who found her, so I'm sure the police will want to talk to me when they arrive."

He nodded but she could see how displeased he was at that.

CHAPTER FOUR

THE SUN WAS FALLING LOW IN THE SKY WHEN THE POLICE arrived. Anthony led two men towards the tower. Peter Mitchell was the local constable in Auldkirk. Last week, after Thea arrived there, she had asked him if he could find information about James Poyntz. Despite Mr. Poyntz being a journalist—someone in a public job—he was practically a ghost and Constable Mitchell found very little about him.

Another man followed behind them. He was probably a bit older than Inspector Thayne and wore a dark blue suit.

"My lord, my lady," the constable bowed his head to her and her uncle. "This is Detective Inspector John Anderson from Edinburgh. He was here visiting when the call came in." Her uncle shook the inspector's hand. "Inspector, this is Lord Ravenholm and his niece, Lady Theodora."

"Visiting?" Uncle Malcolm asked the younger man.

"My mother-in-law lives in Auldkirk, my lord," he replied, smiling pleasantly. "It's a pleasure to meet you both. I wish it was under better circumstances."

"Yes," her uncle agreed, "As do I."

"So you were the one who found the body?" the constable asked her uncle.

Thea shook her head. "I found the bits of fabric wedged in the wall and then brought them out here."

"Once I discovered what was in the wall, I didn't touch anything," Malcolm said.

The constable nodded.

"If you'll show us where, my lord."

Her uncle motioned them forward. As they moved, they kicked the dust and mildew into the air, making it feel near impossible to breathe. The dirt tickled inside her nose. Thea sneezed.

"Father," Anthony said as the three men started to head away, "should I take Thea back to the house?"

Malcolm nodded but looked to the two policemen. Constable Mitchell nodded. "I think that would be best, my lord."

And then the men headed up the stairs.

Anthony placed a hand on her back as he guided her outside. Thea couldn't help but feel a bit resentful that they were going to shove her to the side like she was just a child to be protected.

"I'm going upstairs to freshen up," Thea told him. Her clothes felt grimy and she couldn't wait to get them off. She would love to take a bath but doubted she had the time.

Anthony nodded.

Bridget, the young maid who had been serving her since she arrived in Scotland, was stroking the fire when Thea got into her room.

"My lady." The girl jumped back when she saw her. "I didn't realize you were here."

Thea shook her head as she started on the tiny buttons of her blouse. "Please get me some clean clothes."

"Of course, my lady."

Bridget helped pull layer after dusty layer off. "My lady, if you don't mind me asking, what happened?"

"I went in the East Tower."

The girl's eyes went wide at the mention of the place. Thea sighed.

"I take it you believe it's haunted too?"

"Not quite, my lady. But some of the other servants do."

"Then what is it?"

Bridget looked away, holding the skirt up so Thea could slide into it. "The night that everyone heard the commotion at the tower was the night that Kate disappeared. Lord Ravenholm checked the tower and they found some blood up there but nothing else." Bridget shuddered. "Kate was one of the other maids."

Thea swallowed at that. She knew who Kate was. She had always wondered what happened to her but no one seemed to know.

Kate had always been kind to her, bringing Thea anything she wanted, from biscuits and milk in the middle of the night to a nice steaming pot of tea.

"Were you there that night?"

The girl nodded.

"And no one has heard from Kate since?"

Bridget shook her head. "I wrote to her mother. I thought she might have gone home. She talked about leaving to get married.

Thea had the nagging suspicion that it was Kate's body in the tower. The thought made her stomach turn.

"Do you think something happened to her?" the maid asked as she stopped abruptly in the doorway, the worry for her friend showing clearly in her eyes.

"I hope not."

But inside, she found it unlikely that Kate was okay.

AFTER SHE FINISHED CLEANING UP, THEA WENT BACK TO THE drawing room. Bridget told her that the policemen asked for the staff to wait downstairs in the servants' hall while the family was to wait in the drawing room. The policemen would talk to everyone. Anthony paced by the window, staring out across the grounds.

Thea took a seat on the couch beside Charlie.

"I can't believe this is happening," her cousin groaned. "Why would anyone want to kill someone here?"

Thea rolled her eyes. She doubted the killer had cared much about the location.

The killer probably assumed that no one would find the hidden spot and it might be years or decades before the body was found.

Perhaps it hadn't even been anyone who lived at Ravenholm...

Thea wished that Wilhelmina Livingston was there. The woman she befriended on the train had been an invaluable help when Thea had been trying to find who framed Molly. Her friendship with Wilhelmina had been surprising. On first glance, the young American heiress couldn't have been more different than Thea. However, she had been willing to help Thea in any way she could to clear Molly.

It took hours before the constable and the inspector came back into the house. By then, the occupants of the room had grown restless and Thea wished that she had found the body earlier in the day so that maybe the policemen would be done interviewing everyone and would allow her to go upstairs. The only thing she cared about at the moment was sleep.

Charlie had fallen asleep hours ago, bundled in a blanket as her head rested delicately on the arm of the couch.

"We're sorry to have kept everyone waiting," Constable

Mitchell announced to the room. Thea nudged her cousin awake and the girl woke with a jolt. "We'll try to make this quick and any other questions can be answered in the morning."

Thea barely held back a groan.

CHAPTER FIVE

"MEOW!"

It took everything in Thea not to scream as the sound moved closer.

"Meow."

She blinked awake. The kitten from yesterday stood on her chest, greenish-blue eyes almost glowing in the early morning light. It wore a blue satin ribbon around its neck.

"Good morning, my lady," Bridget said as she threw open one of the curtains. "I hope you slept well."

"I did."

"Are you all right after yesterday? I can get a breakfast tray if you'd rather eat alone this morning. No one would be upset if you didn't want to go down to breakfast."

Thea forced a smile onto her face. "Thank you but I'm perfectly fine." She sat up and the kitten hissed in protest. "Do you know why this cat is here?"

The maid frowned. "He's not yours, my lady? One of the other maids thought…"

She trailed off, looking at the kitten.

Thea shook her head and tried to sit up. "I found it… him yesterday in the Tower. I don't know the first thing about cats."

Bridget grinned. "What's there to know? I gave him some cream downstairs but cats mostly take care of themselves. And that one seems to like you."

Thea looked down at the kitten, who had curled up on the bed near her knee. He didn't seem too bad. Definitely not as vicious as her grandmother's cat. At the very least, Thea didn't think he'd try to bite her anytime soon.

"I suppose you need a name," she told the kitten as she reached down to scratch behind his ear. She thought that cats like that but she wasn't entirely sure. "I don't want to keep calling you 'he' all the time." She glanced up at Bridget. "Any suggestions?"

The maid shook her head. "Perhaps something you read? Or maybe you could name him after someone?"

Thea shrugged. "I honestly have no idea. I'm not very good at naming things. One time my father told me to name a hunting dog. Two week later, I still didn't have a name"—Bridget laughed—"so Father decided to call him 'Neptune.' The next three he named Jupiter, Hercules, and Vulcan."

She eyed the tiny creature quietly purring. There was something almost relaxing about the repetitive motion of scratching his ears. She would worry about naming him later. She slid her feet to the floor and the kitten wailed in protest as she stopped scratching.

Could the person in the wall be Kate? It seemed too preposterous a theory to ask the investigating police that.

Thea moved to her desk. She retrieved a blank page from her draw and quickly wrote a note to send to Inspector Thayne.

THEA FOUND HER AUNT IN THE DRAWING ROOM AFTER breakfast. The Countess was stitching a project in an embroidery hoop and paid little attention as Thea entered the room. Thea sat down in one of the chairs across from her. After a few minutes of saying nothing, her aunt lowered the hoop and looked up.

"How are you doing this morning?" Aunt Diana asked. She looked tired, like she had been up half of the night.

"I'm doing well. I was wondering if we could invite Baron Thayne and his family to the hunt," Thea said softly. "I know it's rather last minute."

"We can. Is there any particular reason why?"

She could feel her face color a little.

"His son is the inspector I met on the train," she told her aunt. "We've been corresponding ever since."

"I see." From her aunt's smirk, Thea knew her excuse worked. Though it wasn't much of an excuse. She really did want to see him again. "I'll write to them immediately."

"Thank you," she murmured but her cheeks burned.

Her aunt smiled at her and Thea turned to leave the room. As she headed towards the library, Mr. Semple was in the hall. She pulled the letter addressed to Inspector Thayne from her pocket.

"Will you put this in the post today?" Thea held the letter out to him.

The butler bowed his head. "Of course, my lady."

"Thank you." She smiled at him and continued on her way.

AFTER LUNCH, THEA WENT BACK TO HER ROOM. THE KITTEN napped on the small pile of pillows and blankets that Bridget constructed that morning. The sunlight streamed through the windows. His fur, which had looked just gray the first time she saw it, appeared to have strands of black and white scattered throughout.

When he heard her, his head popped up and he let out a cry, almost like he was afraid that she wouldn't pay attention to him.

"I see you," she whispered gently.

She reached a tentative hand out to him. He bumped his head into her fingers and she couldn't stop the laugh that bubbled up from her lips.

"I see you found my glove."

"Meow," the kitten said with a proud smile, twisting to rub his cheek against her hand.

Fortunately for her, they weren't a favorite pair. They were cream crochet, made by her friend Louise but the style was not her favorite and the fabric sported many errors, including the fact that the right hand nearly doubled the left. She never had the heart to get rid of them.

However, if they were going to a good home with the little thief, well, that was completely acceptable.

She plucked the other off of the vanity where he had clearly found the first and presented it to him.

A knock on the open door sent Thea spinning. Anthony stood in the doorway. "May I come in?"

"Of course."

He walked inside, his expression grim. "I thought you might like to know that Constable Mitchell and the inspector from last night are back."

"Oh?"

"Inspector Anderson plans to attend the hunt. There was a maid that disappeared six years ago during the hunt, and the Inspector thinks that might be her since no one's ever heard from her and the body looks like it's been there awhile."

That made sense. The same people often attended the annual hunt. It had been her father's favorite event. Ever since her father's death, Thea had purposely missed it. She either left Ravenholm earlier or arrived later in September. Her mother avoided it entirely now.

This year, Thea decided she needed to move forward. It was just her luck that the event would be marred by yet another death.

"I thought you ought to know." He reached out a hand, letting the kitten sniff at it before he reached under the cat's chin. The kitten purred loudly. "Are you doing all right?" Anthony stared at her, his tone soft as he spoke. "It can't be easy finding another body."

Thea stiffened, hoping her expression gave nothing away. To be honest, she had been focused on trying to identify the body.

"Do you think it's Kate?" she asked. No one had actually said, beyond that it was a young woman in a maid's dress. She and Bridget suspected, since the time frame of Kate's disappearance seemed right, but another maid could have gone missing during that time.

He hesitated and the kitten whined until Anthony resumed his movements. "Yes. I'm surprised you remember her."

"She indulged me. She wasn't that much older than me."

His expression grew grim and he glanced away. "I know."

She had forgotten that Anthony and Kate were about the same age.

Anthony smiled but it was pained, his eyes suspiciously bright. He gave the kitten one last scratch under his chin and the kitten whimpered as Anthony pulled his hand back and left abruptly.

Thea watched him go, her brow furrowing as she rubbed the spot behind the kitten's ears. He didn't seem to understand why Anthony had run off either.

Thea didn't think that a family member would have been so cruel as to stuff a person in the wall. Could a staff member have done it? Or perhaps a guest had been the culprit.

Maybe she could find the staff and guest lists from six years ago. She would ask Bridget to help.

CHAPTER SIX

The dressing gong rang only minutes before but Thea was rather surprised that Bridget wasn't in there preparing her evening gown.

"I found the guest lists, my lady," Bridget said instead of a greeting after she closed the door. "I'm sorry I'm late, my lady. I had to copy them."

Thankfully, it was just a family dinner tonight. There was no need to dress anywhere near as fancy as she would during the hunt. Not that she minded dressing nicely but they didn't have the time tonight to redo her hair and for her to change her clothes, so she opted just to change into a new dress. The simple hair style she had worn during the day would suffice.

Bridget passed the guest lists to her as she made her way to the wardrobe. One list was from six years ago and the second was the current guest list.

Thea took a look and was surprised by the number of names she recognized on the list from six years ago.

"My lady," Bridget said softly, drawing her out of her thoughts.

Thea tucked the lists into her journal inside the desk drawer. She would take a better look at them later.

The dress that Bridget had selected for her was a muted shade of green with ivory lace and black netting. Simple but elegant. Unlike most of her other evening dresses, it was barely trained. It was ideal for a small family dinner.

Bridget stood by the vanity, frowning. She held up one of the shiny star hairpins, part of a set of two. It would be the perfect thing to pin down the couple of stray hairs that came loose during the day. "My lady, did you move the other hairpin?"

Thea shook her head. "It's not over there?"

"I saw it a moment ago." She got to her knees and searched under the vanity. Thea blinked. Where could it have gone? The way the maid was acting, it seemed like she thought she'd be blamed for stealing but why would she take something so trivial and then point out that it was missing?

"It will show up eventually."

Bridget glanced up, staring at Thea for a second before she stood. "I can look for it while you're at dinner."

Thea waved her hand. "Really, it's fine. I'm sure it'll turn up." The kitten meowed loudly in agreement from his perch on the desk chair. "See? He thinks so too."

The maid smiled, though it didn't meet her eyes. Her hands trembled and she clutched at her apron.

The kitten preened as Thea reached out and scratched his head before she pulled her gloves on and left for dinner.

"How are you?" Uncle Malcolm asked Thea as she walked into the drawing room. She was tired of hearing that question. It was like they thought she was going to break down at any moment.

"I'm doing well." She smiled and hoped it didn't look too forced.

Her uncle nodded. When it became clear he wasn't going to say anything else, she moved past him to sit beside Charlie, who had her nose stuck inside the evening paper.

"What are you reading?" she asked.

"Mr. Poyntz's latest article about the monoplane. Apparently, it's an all-Scottish powered aircraft."

Thea blinked. Charlie said that like it was significant. "Is that not normal?"

Charlie shook her head. "The ones I've read about have been made elsewhere or are gliders. Everything about it is so fascinating."

"I didn't know you were a fan of James' work," Aunt Diana said as she sat down on the couch beside them.

"James?" Thea whipped her head around to face her aunt.

"I was presented with his aunt, Helen."

From Charlie's expression, it was clear she hadn't known.

"You would have met him when he was here. It's been years now but he came with Helen and Neville for the hunt one year."

"I don't remember," Charlie said softly.

"Well, you were young at the time. You probably didn't see much of him. He's supposed to come this year, so you can discuss his work with him then."

CHAPTER SEVEN

THE NEXT MORNING, THE DOORKNOB CLICKED OPEN AND A second later, Bridget came in carrying a silver tray with envelopes as Thea wrestled her silver hairbrush away from the kitten. During the night, the kitten had a fit of destructiveness, scratching the legs of the chairs and undoing the ribbons on her braid and tangling her hair into knots. Thea had caught him trying to make off with a bejeweled hatpin. She stopped him, for fear of him hurting himself, and he gave that up without a fight. The hairbrush though, he had decided that was his and he was not going to let go, howling loudly as Thea tried to pry his paws from the brush handle.

"It's bigger than you!" she exclaimed. "What do you even want it for? I actually need it."

As it was, she wasn't sure she'd be able to get the knots out without cutting the hair off.

The kitten let out a loud wail and finally released the brush. She glared at the kitten. He gave her the most miserable look that made her feel like she was a monster. But she wouldn't feel guilty.

"Mr. Semple asked me to bring you your mail, my lady." The maid smiled brightly, even as Thea rubbed her eyes.

"Thank you," she said, reaching for them. The kitten swiped at the tray, following the shiny metal as Bridget took it away. Thea knew she should get dressed but she was too curious to see what the envelopes held.

The first letter that she opened was from Mr. Poyntz. His jerky, sharp-edged writing clearly came from taking notes for articles. Like his other letter, it was short and to the point. He didn't waste time with pleasantries, opting instead to get as much information across with the bare minimum of words. It was almost like he was sending a telegram. Briefly, Thea wondered if he sent many telegrams. It would explain the way he wrote.

Lady Theodora,
I would be delighted to speak with your cousin about the articles. I'm glad that someone likes them. I will be at Ravenholm Castle Thursday.
J.P.
P.S. I heard about the murder. Do not get involved.

Thea rolled her eyes before she could help herself. How did he even hear about it? Constable Mitchell said that they were keeping that news quiet until they had a suspect. How curious that a newspaper man managed to hear about it so quickly.

She set that one down and reached for the other letter. The now familiar crest of Clan Thayne was pressed into the wax seal on the back and she popped the envelope carefully open. Inspector Thayne's handwriting made for a sharp contrast to Mr. Poyntz's. It was still more utilitarian than you would expect a gentleman's handwriting to be. However, he had added some small flourishes that Mr. Poyntz neglected completely, such as signing his name instead of just initials.

Dear Lady Thea,
I hope you are doing well, despite your troubling news.
Thank you for informing me of the situation there. My mother
received an invitation for our family to attend the hunt at Raven-
holm this weekend. I assume that you had a hand in that.
Sincerely,
E. Leslie Thayne

Unlike Mr. Poyntz, Inspector Thayne didn't bother to tell her that she should stay away from the investigation.

"I could take the kitten to my room this morning. It's sunnier up there and there's less things for him to get into. I can bring him back this afternoon." Bridget paused as she tidied up the room. "Was something wrong, my lady?"

"No." Thea looked back down at the letter. "That would be wonderful. Thank you."

"Do you need help with your clothes?"

Thea eyed the simple cotton blouse and skirt that the other girl had laid out. It would be easy enough to get dressed by herself. It wasn't like she was completely helpless without Molly. She shook her head. "No, thank you."

It really wasn't fair to poor Bridget to give her twice the amount of work and present it as a reward. And she still had to help prepare the house for the guests that would be arriving in the next few days.

But the girl just smiled. "I'm happy to help, my lady."

"Really, it's fine. I won't be changing clothes after breakfast."

She opened the drawer to put the letters away and remembered she put the guest lists in her journal. She would look at them later.

IT WASN'T UNTIL AFTER LUNCH THAT THEA FINALLY sequestered herself in her bedroom to look at the lists. It seemed like everyone was afraid of her spending too much time alone. As a result, she was slowly losing her mind.

She pulled the journal with the lists out of the desk drawer. The journal was a worn, well-loved leather-bound book that her father had given to her for her birthday years ago. It contained all the notes she made during her investigation of Daniel Talbot's murder and it seemed only fitting to work out the details of Kate's death there. Perhaps the book was lucky and would help her solve the murder.

She glanced over the list of all the guests from six years ago —1904.

Uncle Malcolm's sister's sons, Ernest and Francis Livingston, were constantly at Ravenholm and it was no surprise to see them on the guest list. Ernest's first wife, Jennie, was there as well. Thea had never made the connection before between cousin Ernest as being Wilhelmina's husband.

Rosamond and Oswald Erskine and their daughters, Camilla and Sylvia were on the list. Camilla, their older daughter had been presented during the same Season as Thea but Camilla had recently married a viscount with a crumbling estate. The younger daughter, Sylvia, had gone to finishing school with Charlie.

Helen and Neville Poyntz were at the hunt, along with their daughter Emma. James Poyntz, their nephew, was there also that year. Emma had attended school with Charlie and Sylvia. Emma's father owned the *West End Gazette*, the newspaper that James wrote for.

Had one of them killed Kate?

A light knock came at the door and she hid the journal and lists in her desk. A second later, Bridget rushed in with the kitten, her eyes wide.

"What's wrong?" Thea asked.

"I went up to my room to check on the kitten." Thea blinked. That didn't seem like it would require the urgency with which the maid had sped into the room. Perhaps he had another fit like he had that morning.

Thea frowned and held her hands out to take the kitten from her.

Bridget continued, "Kate used to share the room with me. Her things were sent to her mother when she disappeared. I've been up there during the day plenty of times before and have never seen anything." Bridget thrusted her finger in the kitten's direction. "But he had my mother's locket and was trying to hide it in a crack in one of the baseboards and that's when I found it!"

"It?"

She nodded. "It was a love letter to Kate. She must have hidden it there. I'd have never noticed it if it wasn't for him."

The kitten lifted his head, his big eyes shining so innocently. Thea shook her head and ran her fingers down his silky fur.

Bridget reached for something tucked into her apron and held out a piece of paper to Thea. It was thin, cheap quality, unlike the paper of the letters she had received. The hand that wrote the letter was clearly self-taught: messy, almost childlike, and blocky. Thea squinted, attempting to decipher it.

"My beloved Kate," she read aloud and paused, looking at Bridget. Someone had clearly fancied the maid and it felt a little uncomfortable to read her personal mail, whether or not they were dead.

Despite the fact that she had never received one, Thea could still recognize it for what it was - a love letter. The man who wrote it spoke of them leaving Ravenholm for good and starting their lives away from there. The whole thing was rather beautiful and she couldn't help but feel a little envious at the idea of being so loved by another person.

The letter's signature was blank.

Who wrote the letter? Had he killed her? If he didn't kill her, did he know she was dead? Perhaps he thought she ran off and left him behind.

"Do you think whoever wrote that killed her?" Bridget asked Thea.

"It's possible."

Thea sighed and stroked the kitten's back. He purred contently from where he'd curled up on her lap.

"Can you see if you can find anything out about it?" she asked.

"Of course, my lady." Bridget bowed her head and left the room.

Thea couldn't help but wonder about Kate's love letter's writer.

CHAPTER EIGHT

THE NEXT MORNING WHEN THEA WOKE UP, HER MIND FELT sharp, awake, and focused. She stood up out of the bed and pulled her dressing gown on, ignoring the kitten's protests as she displaced him on the blanket. His bleary eyes stared up at her.

"Sorry, little one," she murmured, stroking the kitten's head. He shifted and settled under the covers instead. He purred, his eyes falling shut again.

Her mood was lighter as she pushed one of the curtains back to stare out the window.

"My lady! You're up!" Bridget exclaimed as she entered the room.

"Please prepare a bath for me." Bridget nodded. "And then, I'd like to look around your room, if you don't mind. Right after breakfast."

Servants' belongings were inspected, so maybe Kate had hidden other things in odd places that she didn't want found.

The maid blinked. "No. Of course not, my lady. But why?"

"Maybe Kate left something else," Thea said. "It's worth taking a look."

"Yes, my lady." With that, Bridget left the room to go draw her a bath.

———

THE MAIDS' QUARTERS AT RAVENHOLM WERE JUST AS SPARSE AS the ones in Astermore. Not a bit of the upstairs was stuffy or dingy but with a housekeeper as meticulous as Mrs. Campbell, it wasn't entirely surprising. The halls were whitewashed and spotless. Thea imagined that Mrs. Campbell probably had one of the maids scrub the floors every day.

Thea wore the plainest of the dresses she owned to follow Bridget discreetly through the green baize door at the end of her floor and up the servants' stairs to the attic. At that time of the day, most of the servants were out in the main part of the house, cleaning the bedrooms or preparing the dining room for lunch.

When they reached the end of the hallway, Bridget pulled the last door on the right open and shut it quickly behind them as they entered so that no one might come across them accidentally.

"It's not much, my lady," Bridget said as Thea surveyed the room. "This one is mine. That one had been Kate's—" she pointed at the bed by the door "—but Fiona uses it now."

Two iron beds had been made with the same neat corners and a worn woven rug lay on the floor between them. Across from the beds, a large wardrobe dominated the room. A woven basket contained what appeared to be extra linens.

"That last year, Kate disappeared constantly, so no one thought there was anything unusual about it. When she never showed back up, her belongings went to her mother years ago."

Thea nodded.

"There might still be something." Kate hid one letter. Who was to say she didn't hide more?

"Of course, my lady." Bridget stepped back and allowed Thea to pace around the room.

"Has this wardrobe always been here?"

"Yes, my lady."

"Have you searched for anything else Kate might have hidden in there?"

Bridget shook her head but opened the wardrobe doors. She felt along the back and the sides, pressing at the wood at random.

"It might have a false back or a panel," the maid explained when she saw Thea's curious glance before she went back to feeling inside the wardrobe for one of the hiding spots she spoke of.

Thea dropped to her knees and felt under the bed closer to the door. Metal rods were the only thing she found. Thea supposed that wouldn't have been the best hiding spot anyway. Anyone might have turned over the mattress and have been able to find it.

The room was not as barren as one might expect a maid's room to be. Most employers had probably never ventured upstairs but a servant lived in their employer's home. It made sense that they would decorate the space with what personal possessions they had. A vase with fresh flowers sat on one of the windowsills, bringing some color to the room.

"Those were my mother's favorites. She used to have them everywhere. Around the house, in her hair, growing in the window box," Bridget said as she stood up from the wardrobe with one of the drawers, seeing where Thea was staring.

"Were?"

"She died when I was a child. I barely remember her."

"I'm sorry to hear that."

Bridget shook her head. "It's been a long time. Her ladyship allows me to pick some of the flowers from the garden. I don't think I could afford to keep them otherwise." She smiled at the memory.

It had always amazed Thea that her father and her aunt were so different from her grandmother. Prudentia Prescott-Pryce was an intimidating woman but Aunt Diana didn't have the same frightening presence as her mother. When Thea's father was alive, he hadn't either. He had been quiet, sometimes secretive but never menacing. Her grandmother would have never allowed Bridget to pick flowers from the garden.

"I found something underneath the wardrobe," her maid said, snapping Thea out of her thoughts. "I never thought to look under here before."

Bridget stood and held out a parcel of dusty, yellowed paper tied with twine. The papers mentioned the East Tower.

"Treasure?" Bridget asked from where she read over Thea's shoulder. "What treasure?"

"I don't know."

Thea couldn't remember hearing about a treasure in the East Tower. She wondered if her family members knew anything. She folded the papers and tucked them inside the pocket of her skirt. She would study them more later.

The only thing left that Thea could think of to do was to make sure there had been nothing else behind the baseboard. She turned to Bridget and said, "Show me where you found the letter that you brought me yesterday."

THEA HAD JUST SAT DOWN AT HER DESK WHEN SOMEONE knocked on the door. The kitten—she really did need a name for him—crawled into her lap. After calling for the person to come in, the door pushed open to reveal Anthony yet again.

"Please be honest," she quipped, "you keep coming in here to avoid the party preparations."

He held up his hands in the air. "You've caught me."

They laughed and he leaned against the wall by the window.

He chuckled, crossing his arms. "Now it's your turn to tell the truth. You're also avoiding the preparations."

Thea laughed and motioned to her desk. "I was trying to write a letter."

Anthony rolled his eyes. He turned to the window, his shoulder tense. "I can't believe that Kate never ran away."

Thea stared at him.

"Were you two close?" She hadn't thought so but after his reaction the other day, it had been on her mind. Perhaps they had been.

He refused to meet her eyes. "She started here when she was thirteen as a maid but she lived in town before that. We used to see each other around. I caught her sneaking visits in the stables to see the horses." Thea giggled at this, much to Anthony's displeasure. He glared until she stopped. "I thought of her as a friend."

When he finished speaking, Thea could have sworn that she saw tears in his eyes before he turned back to stare out of the window. Anthony forced a smile on his face when he looked back at her but it appeared more like a grimace. "I had hoped that she had found some happiness elsewhere. But I suppose…"

Thea blinked back tears. She hadn't realized that her eyes had started watering. She didn't know that Anthony and Kate had been friends. It was amazing how much one person could affect them all so much.

"I know the two of you were close," he continued. "Didn't she used to be your maid every time you were here?"

She had been. As the maid who had taken care of her

when Thea was too old to need a nurse or a nanny but too young to join into the activities of the grown-ups, Kate spent more time than she probably should have entertaining her. Because of that, everything about finding who had killed Kate felt personal.

Seeing her reaction, Anthony walked over and placed a hand on her shoulder. "Don't worry too much about it. I'm sure Inspector Anderson will get to the bottom of it while he's here."

Thea forced a smile onto her face and ran her fingers down the kitten's back. He purred but otherwise stayed asleep. His weight in her lap was comforting.

She wasn't going to tell her cousin that she was looking for the person who did this. Other than Bridget, no one really seemed like they understood Thea's need for answers.

When she got back into her room after dinner, Thea locked the door, moved to her desk, and opened the drawer where she had stored her journal.

With one of the pens on her desk, she began writing everything that happened the day in the tower. She started with Charlie's story of the haunting.

Thea moved onto how she saw the water and found the piece of fabric wedged in the wall. She wanted to look at everything as objectively as possible but she couldn't do that if what she had learned was just in her head.

On the top of the next page, she wrote 'East Tower' in big letters and listed everything she could recall about the tower. *No detail was too small to not be noted*, she decided. Even the unimportant things might have some significance to figure out what treasure Kate had been looking for.

She would have liked to have asked her family about the

treasure, but it seemed inappropriate to bring it up during dinner since the conversation would most likely turn to the murder.

Thea unfolded the love letter and studied the handwriting. It was probably by a servant who had taught himself how to write. It wasn't by someone who had been tutored, so no one of any means.

The bundle of papers was less than she thought. A few of them looked rather old and were thicker than regular paper. They even smelled old. One was a floor plan of what Thea quickly recognized as the East Tower. Some appeared to be ripped from a book, probably a diary. The last paper was the newest. The handwriting looked masculine. It seemed to be an analysis of where the treasure was.

Her eyes grew heavy. She tucked the papers into her journal and hid it away before she went to sleep.

CHAPTER NINE

"GOOD MORNING!" ANTHONY STOOD UP AT THE TABLE AS THEA walked into the dining room.

"I take it you're feeling better," she said softly. It seemed his previous misery was forgotten. And just in time too. The party would begin tomorrow.

"Much, thank you."

She grinned at him, then headed to the sideboard beside her uncle to get some food. Uncle Malcolm smiled at her and handed her a plate so she could take some food and head to the table.

"Good morning," Uncle Malcolm said as they sat down. "Do you know if Charlie's coming down this morning?"

Charlie had only been down to breakfast a handful of mornings since they had found Kate. On the morning that she joined them, she'd rub at her eyes like she couldn't fully wake up. It was so unlike her to sleep in. Charlie loved to socialize during the hunts. She loved being fawned over by the older women and to stare at whatever young men came to the party. Thea always thought the younger girl would do well during her upcoming Season but lately, she wondered if Charlie wasn't as excited for it as she'd once been.

Thea had always felt awkward during parties. She didn't have much in common with the people attending, even if they were all part of the same social group. She really wished they were more exciting, though this one promised to be interesting. She was also looking forward to seeing Wilhelmina, Mr. Poyntz, and especially Inspector Thayne again.

With so much on her mind, Thea didn't feel like eating right now. She stood as the other two finished their meals. Uncle Malcolm eyed the barely touched plate as they left the dining room.

"Perhaps you should take it easy today," her uncle said in a tone that seemed to assume she felt unwell. "We wouldn't want you to miss out tomorrow."

"Don't worry. I think I'll spend today resting. I still need to select my outfits for the party."

Her uncle grimaced and out of the corner of her eye, she could see Anthony press his lips together to keep from laughing.

"Yes, well, enjoy that." Uncle Malcolm looked pained by the words.

Thea smiled at him, though she knew she had no intention of choosing the dresses she'd wear for the party. She wasn't like Charlie and didn't find the enjoyment that her cousin did in staring at clothing for hours. She planned to meet Bridget back in her room after breakfast. She was determined to figure out who had written the letter to Kate.

The kitten was sunning himself on her desk when Thea walked in. He greeted her with a soft meow but otherwise seemed disinterested in her. She smiled. Despite not being fond of her grandmother's cat, this one had grown on her rather quickly. She lifted him from his spot, ignoring his half-hearted protests that ceased the minute she rubbed his ears.

"Good morning to you, too," she murmured.

Bridget was looking for a list of the staff who had worked in the house when Kate had gone missing. What Thea hadn't expected was for Bridget to walk in carrying a basket of her clean laundry. Immediately, the maid got to work sorting and hanging the appropriate items.

"Did you find out who was here?" Thea asked perplexed. The kitten cried loudly, bumping his head against her hand until she continued scratching.

"Yes, my lady." Bridget leaned down to pick up one of Thea's skirts, only for it to reveal a black, leather-bound book.

"What's this?"

"I took it from Mr. Semple's office," she said a little bit too proudly. She bent and picked up a second book. "And this one is from Mrs. Campbell's rooms."

Thea blinked. She wasn't entirely sure how Bridget had gotten into the butler's and housekeeper's rooms but she wasn't sure she wanted to know either.

"I figured that we could copy them and I could return them when I bring the laundry down."

"All right," Thea said. She could hardly argue with that logic, though she found it odd that the butler and housekeeper left their rooms unlocked. Perhaps things were different at Ravenholm than Astermore.

Bridget sat down, flipping through one of the books. Thea set what she quickly discovered was the housekeeper's book on the desk and pulled her journal out of the drawer. She copied the names from the book down quickly, careful not to leave any marks on the pages. Mrs. Campbell's eyes were sharp from years of detailed work. As a child, Thea had never gotten away with anything when she visited Ravenholm. When she finished, she gently closed the book and handed it back to Bridget, who passed her Mr. Semple's ledger, complete with the employee's positions and salaries.

Thea glanced back at Bridget. She wondered if the maid had looked to see how much the other servants were paid. She had to admit, if she was in Bridget's position, she wouldn't have been able to resist looking.

Mr. Semple and Mrs. Campbell had kept meticulous records of who had worked in the house. She closed the ledger and handed it back to Bridget, who smiled and piled dirty laundry on top of the books in the basket.

"I'll be back shortly, my lady."

Thea nodded. She didn't mind if Bridget took her time. She was going to analyze the names on the list and see if she could make some sort of sense of it all.

***

It was closer to several hours before Bridget returned.

"I'm sorry it took me so long, my lady," the maid apologized. "Constable Mitchell and Inspector Anderson returned and are asking all sorts of questions."

"They asked you questions?"

Bridget nodded. "They wanted to know more about Kate since I shared a room with her. They were going to look around to see if they could find anything. They'll probably want to talk to you again too, my lady."

"Probably." They mostly left her alone that night, asking only the bare minimum. They probably assumed that the whole experience would be too traumatizing for her.

The maid shook her head. "I overheard them say it. They thought it was suspicious that you weren't afraid of the tower being haunted."

Thea rolled her eyes and pressed her lips together. She hoped that these policemen were more capable than Inspector Stanton from the train, whose sole purpose of investigating Mr.

Talbot's murder had been to frame Molly for killing her husband.

"I'll wait until they call for me. After all, why would I know that they want to talk to me?" She smiled at Bridget and motioned for the maid to come beside her. "In the meantime, let's see if we can't narrow down this list."

Bridget walked behind her, standing over Thea's shoulder.

"He was probably a footman," Bridget said, pointing at the names on the list. Thanks to Bridget's snooping abilities, they knew exactly who was in the house the day that Kate disappeared. Mrs. Campbell had even marked down in her book the date that Kate went missing as a note to look for a new housemaid.

"What makes you say that?"

Bridget raised a brow at her, a smirk on her lips. "Mr. Semple is ancient, my lady."

Thea giggled a little at that. The butler wasn't ancient but he was definitely old enough to be her father.

"Kate always made comments about men. She liked tall men with strong arms."

Thea laughed. That described all of the footmen at Ravenholm: all matched over six feet tall and all were nice enough to look at.

But then she was struck with a sudden burst of inspiration.

"Could you collect some writing samples from the footmen?"

Bridget's brow furrowed. "Writing samples?"

"You could have them write a note for Kate's mother. Then we'd have their handwriting and could compare it to the love letter."

The maid's eyes went wide. "That's brilliant, my lady!"

A knock on the closed door startled them both. Thea shoved her journal into the drawer and replaced it with a half-finished letter to Molly before she nodded at Bridget to get the door. Mrs. Campbell stood in the hall.

"The police wish to see Lady Theodora," the housekeeper told Bridget. "They're in the drawing room."

Thea rose from her chair, holding on tightly to the kitten.

As she entered the drawing room, she saw Aunt Diana sitting in one of the large chairs. The policemen both stood by the fireplace.

"Gentlemen, is there something I can do for you?" Thea asked as carefree as she could manage.

"I'm not sure if you remember us," Inspector Anderson said. "I'm Detective Inspector Anderson from Edinburgh and this is Constable Mitchell."

"Yes, I remember."

The inspector nodded and they all sat down. The younger man pulled out a notebook as Constable Mitchell sat down next to him. The kitten settled into Thea's lap.

"Everyone we've spoken to said that the tower was thought to be haunted. Lady Charlotte said you wanted to go in. Why?"

"I always used to go out there. I like the view of the loch," Thea said simply.

"But you hadn't been in it in six years?" Thea shook her head. The inspector frowned. "Why did you go inside?"

"I didn't believe that the tower was haunted. We used to spend time there when we were children."

A medieval tower was the perfect place to play and dream. It always sounded more romantic when they called it that, instead of the East Tower.

He nodded again and jotted something down.

"Why did you go upstairs?"

She tried not to fidget under his gaze but the kitten let out a wail. She ran her fingers through his fur until he calmed down. The inspector stared at the kitten but Thea didn't react. "Lady

Charlotte said that there was a ghost upstairs. I've never actually seen a ghost before."

"What made you look inside the fireplace?"

"I saw a pool of water there and went to take a look around."

More scribbles.

"I think that'll be all for me. Constable, do you have any questions?" Constable Mitchell shook his head and both men stood. "Thank you for your help, Lady Theodora."

Thea watched them both leave and she sighed a breath of relief they were gone.

CHAPTER TEN

It was just after lunch when Bridget returned with the letters to Kate's mother. She laid them across the desk and stepped back.

"How are you going to be able to tell, my lady?"

"I'm hoping that some of it will look the same. Like this." Thea pointed to the slanted way that the lowercase T had been crossed, then to the Ts on the letter. They didn't match at all.

"Oh. I see," the maid said softly. "Would you like me to help or...?"

"It's fine if you leave. I know I've taken up a lot of your time."

Bridget grimaced. "I want to know what happened to Kate."

"I'll let you know if I find anything," Thea promised. "You should get back before Mrs. Campbell misses you."

"Yes, my lady."

Bridget left. The door clicked softly behind her.

Finding the matching handwriting proved to be more difficult than Thea expected. She supposed it probably wasn't the most viable way to find out who Kate's admirer was but it was really all she had to go on. It was hard to piece anything together six years after the fact.

She had almost given up on the idea when she found a 'B' that matched the one in the 'beloved' before Kate's name. What was even odder was that the condolence letter was written in what she assumed was Scottish. She wished she could read it but the letters matched almost exactly. The way the words flowed was only slightly more polished but still not nearly as confident as someone who had been taught how to write properly.

She looked to the signature at the bottom, only to discover that it was nearly illegible.

Thea felt a bit like screaming. She barely refrained from doing so, closing her eyes and taking a deep breath. As far as obstacles went, it could have been worse. The other letters were clearer to read. She reached for her pen to make a list of the names but the pen wasn't where she had left it last night.

That's strange. Perhaps Bridget had moved it when she cleaned the desk?

But the rest of the papers on top of the desk were in order. She glanced beneath the desk—perhaps it had been knocked to the floor—but nothing. Thea pulled the large drawer in the center open but the pen she was looking for wasn't in there either. How odd... the pen wasn't worth stealing. It was a relatively cheap fountain pen, the kind you gave to a child. It looked like a thousand other fountain pens. It only really held any value to her. Her father gave it to her when she was younger, so why would anyone bother taking it?

Thea shook her head and dug around in the drawers until she came across another pen that still had ink and started her list of names from the letters. Six letters from the footmen but only five legible signatures: Allan, Duncan, Ewen, Gordan, and Ralph.

That only left Neil Thomson. How would he know if

Kate's mother could read Scottish or not if he didn't have knowledge of her family?

He couldn't.

Thea smiled. She had the answers to one mystery. Maybe he had answers to some of the others.

Which one was Neil Thomson? She was embarrassed to say that she couldn't tell the footmen apart. The ones at Ravenholm were all tall, handsome, nameless figures to her, unlike the ones at Astermore.

She grew up seeing the boys who became Astermore's footmen. Some were only a few years older than her. It was the same with the maids. The manor provided many jobs for the people who lived in the town and the residents of the manor relied on them.

She decided she wouldn't say anything until Bridget came to help her change for dinner. After all, there wasn't much she could do at the moment. Until then, she would work on her embroidery.

———

THERE WERE FEW RELATIONSHIPS MORE PERSONAL THAN THAT between master and servant. Despite the fact that Molly had her own secrets when she had been Thea's maid, she had still been one of Thea's closest friends. Whatever Bridget's past was that allowed her to comfortably steal the ledgers and lie to those she worked with, Thea didn't need to know it. Not now, maybe not ever. They were united in finding Kate's killer.

"I think the letter was written by Neil," she told the maid.

Bridget looked between the love letter and the note Neil had written. "I think you're right, my lady."

She set the letters down on Thea's desk. "Can you point him out to me later? I'd like to speak to him, tonight if possible."

"Of course, my lady." Bridget hesitated by the desk.

"Is something wrong?" Thea asked as she reached up to clasp her necklace.

"I found a key on the floor earlier. I set it down on the desk…"

"And now it's gone," Thea finished.

Bridget looked up at her in horror. "You don't think," she started hesitantly, glancing around, afraid of being overheard. "You don't think this room's haunted, do you?"

Thea scoffed. "There's no such thing as ghosts."

Bridget shifted. "Something's been making things move and disappear. I found one of your scarves on the floor by the bed this morning after you left for breakfast. It had been in the wardrobe."

That was harder to explain. Things disappeared. People misplaced things all the time. But objects didn't move themselves.

"What was the key for?"

The maid's brow furrowed. "I don't actually know. I found it by the fireplace. I assumed it was yours." Thea frowned. "It was a small gold key. I thought it might be your trunk key."

Thea moved across the room. She had left the trunk key in a box on the vanity table. Yet, sure enough, it was missing. She sighed and closed the lid of the box again. When she turned around, the blood had completely drained from Bridget's face.

"There is a ghost!"

"I'm sure there's a logical explanation for everything."

Bridget shook her head, her movements frantic. "It all started right after you found Kate. It's her ghost. She's angry with all of us."

That seemed unlikely. For one, ghosts weren't real. For another, everything that had moved or gone missing was all so irrelevant. When they were little, Thea and her brother Cecil used to take turns hiding their father's account ledgers and unimportant correspondence to force him to step out of his study.

Thea didn't believe it was a ghost at all. But she had no explanation of who was actually committing the acts.

———

THEA PULLED AT A THREAD ON THE NAPKIN UNTIL THE HEM started to unravel. It was better than the alternative of drumming her fingers or tapping her foot beneath the table. She didn't know why she felt so nervous. It shouldn't be dangerous. She shouldn't have any trouble from Neil.

At least, she hoped not.

Once dinner ended and they left the dining room, Thea caught a glimpse of Bridget standing out of the way in the hallway. She motioned to Thea, so she broke away from the others.

"I saw Neil leave the house earlier," the maid told her once they were out of the others' earshot, "and followed him to the gardens."

"He's still there?"

Bridget nodded.

Sure enough, they found him in the darkened garden, sitting on one of the benches inside the tall hedges, clutching a rose. It wasn't just any rose. It was the famous Auldkirk rose, pale blush on the inside with white tips. The tenth Earl of Ravenholm had commissioned it for his sweetheart nearly two centuries ago. Sadly, she died on the eve of their wedding. After that, he had the garden filled with them. They were more hardy than regular roses and were the only flower that grew at Ravenholm.

Neil jumped to his feet as he saw them, wiping his cheeks quickly with his shirt sleeve. The rose fell forgotten onto the bench. "My lady! My apologies. This isn't what it looks like."

"You and Kate were close?" she asked.

He started, before he nodded slowly.

"We found your letter to her," Bridget told him.

His mouth opened slightly, his brow furrowing in confusion. "I don't know what you're talking about."

"It wasn't signed but it was clear you wrote it."

Even in the moonlight, Thea could see the flush cross over his face, his eyes flashing in anger. "Was that why you collected letters to send to Kate's mother? To find out who had written to her?"

Thea held up her hands like he was a horse that might startle. "I asked her to collect the letters. I wanted to know if you knew anything about what happened."

The fury on his face disappeared, only to be replaced by a small frown. "My lady?"

"Bridget and I have been looking into what happened." Out of the corner of her eye, she could see Bridget duck her head. "I know it's probably hard for you to talk about but could you tell us anything you remember from before she went missing?"

"From before she was killed, you mean?" he asked, bitterness snapping in his voice. From his reaction, Thea didn't think he had killed Kate. "The inspector already questioned me about it."

Bridget stepped forward and squeezed his hand. "We're not your enemy, Neil. We want to know what happened to her. She was my friend and I always wondered. I hoped that finding some answers could help."

The fight faded from his body, his shoulders drooping as he swayed slightly. Thea took a seat on the bench and motioned for him to sit beside her. He picked up his neglected rose, twirling it between his fingers.

"These were her favorite. The story was just so tragic. She always cried when she heard it but she loved listening to it."

Tears glistened on his face in the moonlight. He fished a locket from under his collar. It was relatively cheap looking on an ordinary chain.

"I gave this to Kate as a promise that we'd be together. The Inspector found it on her body. That's how they knew it was her."

Thea couldn't imagine thinking that the person you loved most in the world had abandoned you for six years only for them to be dead. No wonder Neil was a mess. She would be too.

"You should have this," Bridget said, holding out the letter to him. Thea hadn't even realized the maid had taken it from her desk.

Neil took it, unfolding the paper carefully. He brought it to his face, closed his eyes, and he took a breath. His shoulders fell and his lips drooped into a deep frown. "Is it foolish that I thought I might smell her perfume?"

Bridget shook her head. "I kept the bottle she had opened. It mostly evaporated but I sealed it tight enough that maybe…"

She trailed off, and Neil smiled at her.

"Thank you." He breathed deeply, and Thea felt a little like she was intruding on something deeply personal. "I loved her once. For years, I thought she had abandoned me but now…"

He clenched his hand tightly around the stem of the flower. Thea imagined it had to be painful since the roses still had thorns but Neil didn't seem to care.

"Why is your name 'Neil?'" Thea asked, hoping to distract him if even for a minute.

He blinked as he stared at her. "My lady?"

"Their surname is McNeil," she said, gesturing towards the house. Neil nodded slowly, as if he was wondering what that had to do with anything.

"My mother worked here before I was born and named me for them. My parents met here. When my parents were married, instead of sending them both away, Lord Ravenholm promoted my father to be his valet."

"Oh," Thea said lamely, blushing as she looked down. "I didn't realize."

"Lord and Lady Ravenholm are good people." Neil smiled. His eyes flickered towards Bridget. "They've given many of us a second chance."

Thea frowned. "What do you mean?"

"There was a rumor years ago, my lady, about Mr. Semple. That he had a dark past." He glanced away from them. "I'm not sure if it was true. Kate was the one who told me."

Thea stared at him.

"Do you think Mr. Semple had something to do with her disappearance?"

It was hard to picture. He had always been so kind to her. She hated to think of him being a murderer.

Beside Neil, Bridget had gone pale.

He shook his head. "I don't think so." Neil frowned, twirling the flower between his hands. "She wanted us to go away together, to start our life away from here but I wanted to keep working. I wanted to save some money first." He looked away but Thea could see tears shimmering in his eyes again. "She said she had an idea to get money but wouldn't tell me how."

He rubbed his eyes with his sleeve again. Thea pulled out her handkerchief and passed it to him. He clenched it tightly between his fingers, until his knuckles went white.

"Thank you for telling me this. I'm very sorry for everything you've been through."

Thea squeezed his hand and stood. Bridget was already outside the hedges, moving towards the house before she collapsed against the wall.

"Why wouldn't she have told me about Neil?" the maid whispered. "I thought we were friends." She buried her face in her hands. "How was I so blind? How did I not see any of it?"

Thea reached out and Bridget fell against her, sobbing into her shoulder. When the maid realized what she had done, she pulled away and staggered backwards into the wall. "I'm sorry, my lady. I shouldn't have. It was inappropriate."

"I can hardly blame you or Neil. You've both been through so much. It's had to have been hard to find out the way you did."

"I didn't want it to be her. I hoped it was someone else. Is that horrible of me?"

"I think it's rather human of you," Thea whispered. "Sometimes the ones closest to us hide the most."

She didn't miss the way that Bridget swallowed heavily at that.

CHAPTER ELEVEN

THE NEXT MORNING, THE HOUSE WAS ABUZZ WITH SERVANTS scurrying to complete everything before the guests arrived. Last minute preparations had to be finished, rooms had to be readied, and everything needed to be perfect, especially with a possible murder suspect amongst the guests. Inspector Anderson was already there and waiting.

Thea could barely hide her excitement at the prospect of questioning the guests. She had tucked the kitten into her jacket pocket that morning—he was tiny enough that he fit comfortably inside—and headed downstairs. She was especially looking forward to talking to Mr. Poyntz and getting some answers from him.

Unfortunately for her, he was not the first to arrive.

Instead, it was Charlie's giggling friend, Sylvia Erskine, and her parents, Rosamond and Oswald. She didn't have any particular reason to dislike the Erskines. Most of her aggravation with them came from the fact that every time she saw them, Mrs. Erskine would ask Thea if she was married or engaged yet. Sylvia laughed in the background and grated on Thea's nerves rather quickly.

The next to arrive was Mr. Poyntz and his family in a rather shiny, new automobile. He climbed down from the back of the vehicle and smiled brightly as he saw her.

"Lady Theodora," he greeted, ignoring the way his family stared. "It's a pleasure to make your acquaintance again so soon."

"The pleasure is mine, Mr. Poyntz."

"After I've settled in, would you tour the grounds with me?"

"Of course." Thea pressed her lips together, anxious to know why he wanted to speak to her now. He'd said nothing of importance since the last time they spoke in person. His letters were practically censored. What did he want from her? What was his angle?

"And then later, perhaps I can speak with Lady Charlotte about the monoplane. Assuming she's still interested, that is."

"She's definitely still interested." Charlie had talked of nothing else. In fact, Thea was certain that she'd spent the last several days pouring over the magazines and articles that detailed the plane instead of sleeping. It was hardly a passing fancy for her.

Charlie wanted to be able to build an airplane but the world wasn't quite ready for a lady becoming an engineer for such a contraption. The world had enough trouble with the idea of flying as it was.

"Then I look forward to speaking with her," Mr. Poyntz said before he followed his aunt and uncle into the house.

Thea could hear his cousin teasing him about Thea as they walked inside. Emma Poyntz was nearly as troublesome as Sylvia, though Thea imagined with Mr. Poyntz around this year, the girl would probably be worse. At other parties in past years, she had given Thea many problems. Not for the first time, Thea wished she had made the connection between the Poyntz family and James before. She felt like she would have been better prepared for this if she had known.

Charlie acted much more mature when she wasn't around either of the other girls. Not that Thea could say such a thing without being viewed as cruel, or worse, jealous.

Shaking her head, Thea followed the others inside the house.

———

STROLLING THE GROUNDS WITH MR. POYNTZ WAS NOT NEARLY as awkward as Thea expected. It was strange how comfortable she was around him, like she had known him for longer than she had. The kitten didn't acknowledge Mr. Poyntz's presence, snoring softly from his resting place in Thea's pocket.

Thea and Mr. Poyntz walked arm in arm, and for a few moments, it felt like she didn't have a care in the world.

"Have you spent much time in Scotland, Mr. Poyntz?" Thea asked, trying for the small talk she was so horrible at.

He paused, their steps coming to a halt as he turned to look at her.

"Please, call me James," he told her, a strange look in his eyes. "I insist."

"In that case, I insist you call me Thea, not Theodora."

A smirk twitched on his lips as they started walking again. "What's your aversion to your full name?"

She glared. "My mother thought she was being clever. She named me after my aunt but swapped the first part of her name for the second. Dorothea for Theodora."

James laughed at that.

"That had to be fun as a child, having such similar names."

Thea shook her head. "I didn't get to see her much. She was American. She travelled the world racing automobiles."

"Was?"

"She died, actually not long before my father."

"Was it… did she crash?" James asked softly.

"She was thrown from a horse and died instantly." Thea glanced away for a moment. It always felt strange to her that a woman who was used to handling something as powerful as an automobile would die in such a mundane sort of way.

She looked back at James. "I'm very sorry to hear that."

"Thank you." Thea pressed her lips together. He reached up and patted her arm. The kitten didn't seem to like that, because he chose that moment to wake and announce his presencc loudly.

James stared at where the sound came from and frowned. The kitten popped his head up, blinking. James blinked back.

"There's a cat in your pocket," he said like she might not have realized that.

Thea laughed. She stroked the kitten's head as she pulled him out of her pocket and into her arms.

"I found him in the tower. He seemed to have been abandoned."

"May I?" James asked. He held his hands out to take the tiny creature. Thea deposited the kitten into his hands and laughed again by how annoyed the kitten managed to look. James petted his head. "Does he have a name?"

Thea shook her head. "I can't figure out one that seems right."

James snickered. "He's a kitten, not a child. He just needs a name to recognize when you're calling him."

The kitten opened his mouth to bite James, but James reached around and scratched his chin. The kitten went from vexed to affectionate in seconds, purring louder than Thea ever heard him.

"So tell me about the maid that was found," James said, changing the subject, even as he continued to play with the cat.

"Her name was Kate."

He stared at her for a moment. "Were you the one who found her?"

Thea nodded.

"And are you conducting your own investigation again?" She stayed silent. "I see. Well, please don't take off after any murderers alone this time."

He said the words like they were a joke but she could see the tension in his eyes. He was worried about her.

"I won't," she promised.

James smiled but she could see how forced it was. "Good. Because I'm sure you'll wind up finding them. I've known hunting dogs less efficient than you." He grimaced as he realized how his words sounded. "I didn't mean it quite like that."

"Then I'll take it in the spirit which it was intended." She pushed a smile onto her face and he snorted.

They continued walking until they made it to the tower. Her stomach twisted at seeing it but James didn't so much as flinch. Instead, he led her towards the bluff overlooking the loch.

"How have you been since the train? It was quite an experience."

Thea laughed. *Experience. That was one word for it.*

"I'm all right. I'd be better if I didn't have to find a replacement for Molly."

"Ah yes," James said, "How is Mrs. Talbot doing?"

Thea glanced away. "I haven't heard from her since I've been here."

"I'm sorry to hear that." James looked at her, an odd expression on his face. "Do you know what Mrs. Talbot plans to do with the child?"

"She's going to raise it, I'm sure."

"I imagine that'll be hard as a woman by herself."

Thea shrugged. "She's strong. I think she's stronger than we ever gave her credit for."

"I believe so."

"Besides, Molly's not exactly the typical society wife. She

and Daniel were a slightly less tragic modern-day Romeo and Juliet."

James raised his eyebrows at her. "I'd hate to see what you consider a truly tragic ending."

Thea laughed but it was bitter and cold. "Molly could have remained in jail, framed for the murder. They might not have discovered she was expecting before they declared her guilty and hung her." Thea squeezed her hands tightly as she thought of the horrible fate her former maid could have suffered. "If they had discovered that she was expecting, they might have postponed her execution until after and then the child would have been given to an orphanage for adoption."

James was quiet for a moment. "I was adopted. My parents never knew why my birth mother gave me up. When I was younger, I wondered if it was for a reason like that."

"Did you ever find out about her?"

"Yes." He smiled. "And I found out why. She was young and unmarried and her parents had other plans for her, which didn't include my father. After I was born, she gave me away and her parents arranged for her to marry someone else." He shrugged. "Her husband tracked me down several years ago. I couldn't have been more than eighteen." He shook his head. "He told me that they had two children together. He told me that if he had known, he would have raised me as his own."

"Did you ever meet her?"

He shook his head. "I couldn't bring myself to do it." His hands clenched, betraying that he wasn't as comfortable as he pretended to be. "I have a brother and sister who have no idea I exist.

Thea stared at him.

"And it's not like I've had a bad life," he continued, "I had a mother and father who loved me very much and an aunt and uncle who were willing to take me in when they died. I've been lucky."

She reached for him, unsure of what she should do but feeling like she should offer him some sort of comfort. She laid her hand on his arm and squeezed it.

"If it makes any difference, if I had another brother out there, I'd like to know about him," she said.

James smiled but there was something a little sad and uncertain in his eyes that remained even as they walked back towards the house.

CHAPTER TWELVE

By the time Thea and James arrived back at the castle, many of the other guests had arrived. Thea passed the kitten off to one of the footmen, who promised to take him downstairs to feed and have him brought back to her room. Inspector Thayne and his family were in the drawing room listening to Great Aunt Mary's mindless chatter with Lady Thayne. At least, Thea assumed that she was Lady Thayne.

Upon seeing them, Inspector Thayne stood. She watched him make his excuses before he broke away from the conversation with Mrs. Erskine and a man she assumed was his brother, Josiah.

"Lady Thea," he greeted with a smile that darkened slightly when he took in her companion. "Mr. Poyntz. It's nice to see you both again."

Thea ducked her head, trying to hide her blush. "Inspector."

Beside her, James' snort was barely disguised. She felt the strangest urge to jerk her elbow into his side, like she had with Cecil when they were younger and weren't around anyone who needed to be impressed. It had been subtle, especially when they had their arms locked together but he had always gotten the message. She wondered if James would too if she were to do that now.

She doubted it.

From the corner of the room, Charlie giggled with Sylvia and Emma. The three of them stared in their direction.

"Inspector," James greeted with a smile. "Did you hear our dear Lady Theodora has found herself wrapped up in another mystery?"

Inspector Thayne's eyes narrowed. "She mentioned there had been a body found. She didn't mention that she had gotten involved with it."

"I never said I was," Thea defended herself, keeping her voice quiet. The last thing she needed was to be the subject of gossip.

James chuckled dryly. "I'd be a poor journalist if I didn't know when someone avoided answering questions."

"Kate was my friend," she told them both. "I need to know what happened to her."

Inspector Thayne nodded. "I understand."

Her stomach twisted as he walked away. She turned to James.

"Why did you say anything about it to him?"

"Because you're clearly not concerned enough about yourself, so someone has to be."

"I never asked you to look out for me. Why do you even care?"

"My mistake," the reporter said dryly. "I'll avoid saving your life in the future."

He turned slightly, spotted Charlie, and then walked over to her. Thea clenched her fist at how quickly she had managed to push everyone away.

Wilhelmina Livingston was a far cry from the woman she had befriended on the train journey to Scotland. Instead, she was back to the woman who Thea had met that first day aboard the *Flying Scotsman*, with that larger-than-life personality. What had happened to the intelligent woman who had helped a stranger find out the truth about what happened to her maid?

The Honorable Ernest Livingston was neither handsome nor honorable. He was dull as a rock with the personality of an ill-tempered horse who would kick and trample you. He was built like a beanstalk: tall, thin and wiry.

His younger brother, Francis, had a perpetual smirk on his face. Whatever oil he used to make his hair lay flat made it greasy. Thea always felt uncomfortable around him and tried to avoid him.

Ernest kept a firm grip on Wilhelmina's arm, as if he thought she might wander off if given the slightest bit of leave. Despite her desire to talk to Wilhelmina, the one person Thea thought might understand why she had to investigate, she didn't dare go near Mr. Livingston. He was not the kind of man she would have envisioned as Wilhelmina's husband.

As the remainder of the guests crowded into the drawing room, she found herself searching the room for Inspector Thayne. When she found him, it felt like her legs moved of their own accord until she stood next to him by the window, away from the others in the room.

"I know you're angry with me," Thea started softly.

"You promised that you'd leave any investigations to the police."

"It's not... I'm not..." She wrung her hands together. "I was mostly questioning my maid."

"Your maid?" he repeated slowly like he didn't understand. She nodded. "What does she have to do with anything?"

"Bridget and Kate shared a room."

Inspector Thayne stared at her for a moment. "How do you know that this Bridget didn't have anything to do with Kate's murder?"

She let out a heavy breath and glanced down. "I don't. But she did get me the lists of names of everyone who was in the house when Kate went missing. The guest list and the staff list, I mean." Thea looked up at him. "She also found a love letter from Neil Thomson to Kate."

"A love letter?" He raised an eyebrow. "Where is it?"

"Bridget gave it back to Neil." She cringed even as she said the words.

Inspector Thayne stared at her. "And you didn't find that the least bit suspicious?"

"I know. I'm sorry." She pressed her lips together and looked away.

She heard him sigh.

"Thea," he whispered, his voice soft. They could have been the only two people in the room at the moment. It felt that way. "I just... I worry about you... worry that something might happen to you. Is that wrong of me?"

She shook her head and longed for privacy to talk.

"I'm sorry," she whispered. Her stomach twisted miserably again. Her hand gripped the ledge as she closed her eyes and willed herself not to cry.

Warm fingers trailed over the back of her hand, cautious and uncertain. She blinked her eyes open and glanced at where their hands met. She turned her hand slightly to close around his thumb, wishing she was brave enough to actually hold his hand in front of the room of people.

Thea looked up at him and his eyes were softer this time when he spoke. "I know."

She refused to move for fear that it might jerk them out of the moment. His hand squeezed hers slightly.

"I won't ask you to promise this time, because I know how

you feel. I've felt that way too. But what I will ask is that you let me in. Please don't try to do this alone, because you're not."

He smiled, a bit hesitant, and she couldn't help but smile back.

"I can do that."

Thea could feel someone's eyes on her and she turned her head slightly.

"What is it?" Inspector Thayne asked softly, keeping still as her eyes slid over.

"Inspector Anderson is watching us."

"You didn't mention in your letter that he'd be staying here."

"I didn't know when I wrote you." The inspector moved closer coming towards them. James watched from across the room with eyes that missed nothing. "He's coming this way."

Inspector Thayne pulled his hand back slowly, his body shielding his movements from the Edinburgh policeman.

"Lady Theodora," the man greeted.

"Inspector Anderson." She watched annoyance flash across his face. His eyes darkened at the mention of his title. "Have you met Detective Inspector Thayne from Scotland Yard?"

Understanding flickered, clear for anyone looking to see. He held out his hand and Inspector Thayne shook it.

"What brings you here, Inspector Thayne?"

"I was invited, before the body was discovered."

The older inspector swallowed. It was amazing to look between the two men. Inspector Thayne was clearly younger and stood taller. His suit was a more expensive quality but they were both roughly the same size. Inspector Anderson seemed to have the weight of the world on his shoulders.

Inspector Anderson straightened up. The tension disappeared from his shoulders. "I see." He glanced back towards the room. "I take it you are the son Lady Thayne thought I'd find fascinating."

Inspector Thayne pressed his lips together, clearly fighting a laugh. "That would be my mother. She's become familiar with several of my colleagues in London. I'm afraid she missed her calling as a detective."

Anderson laughed quietly but the tension in his shoulders returned. It was clear that he didn't know how to act at such an event. Thea doubted he was invited to many house parties.

"Do you want to be kept in the loop about the investigation?"

Inspector Thayne nodded. "I'd appreciate that. Thank you."

The other man nodded. "Of course."

Thea saw James still staring over the older inspector's shoulders. Seeing that he had been caught, he glanced away, as if he could pretend that he hadn't been watching the whole conversation. It appeared that despite their harsh words before, he was still concerned about her. She wondered why.

She knew she should apologize. She was unfair to him but it was hard to know if she could trust him when she didn't know what his motives were. Somehow, they just didn't feel as straightforward as Inspector Thayne's.

INSPECTOR ANDERSON TOOK INSPECTOR THAYNE AWAY TO FILL him in on the investigation. Thea hid in the library. She didn't feel like being social, not after fighting with James.

It was the perfect time to see if she could find any information about the treasure that Kate thought was in the tower. The library was filled with hundreds of years of history, both family history and other. Perhaps one of the books would have some information—or at least a rumor—about a supposed treasure in the tower. But where?

"What are you doing in here?"

Thea jumped as the voice appeared behind her. No one had come in the door. *Had someone been in there the whole time?*

Anthony watched her and Thea shifted uncomfortably under his gaze. "What are *you* doing here? Shouldn't you be mingling with the guests?"

"I saw you come in here."

"How did you get in?" She was still in front of the door. She would have seen him come in.

Anthony frowned slightly. "I'm surprised you don't already know about it." He led her to the shelves on the far wall. He reached underneath the shelf and pressed something. One of the panels silently popped open.

Thea took a step forward and looked in. A narrow passage seemed to span the length of the shelves. Small streaks of light shimmered in the dust.

"I think this was used as some sort of spy hole," he said. "You can watch everything that's going on in the library."

He pushed past her and showed a spot on the wall that you could see through the shelves.

"How did I never find this?"

He shrugged. "You were too focused on the ones that go anywhere. This one just goes from the hall to the library. Not very impressive."

He showed her where the lever to open the door to the hallway was. It might not be the most impressive passage, but it seemed like it would be useful.

"You never did say what you were doing in the library."

Thea sighed, running her hands down her arms. The passage had a chill to it that the rest of the house didn't.

"I was looking for information about the tower. Kate thought there was treasure in it."

Anthony laughed. "That old legend?"

"I think that's why she was killed."

Anthony swallowed hard and opened the door back into the library. Thea followed him.

"What's the legend?"

He sat down on the couch and Thea took a seat beside him, eager.

"The three earls that took responsibility were a father and his two sons. The father was said to have hidden a treasure in the tower."

There was one secret place inside the tower. It would make sense if there were more, especially if they had been designed to act as false hiding places.

"The elder son wanted it and was rumored to have killed his father for it. When his brother found out what had happened, they dueled and the younger one killed the elder."

"Did that really happen?"

Anthony shrugged. "I have no idea. It was two hundred years ago. I know I've seen some old journals in here. Maybe one of them has something about the treasure."

She nodded. "I'll look."

Thea must have been in the library longer than she expected, because when Inspector Thayne found her, she was back to looking through books.

"What are you looking for?"

Thea quickly closed the journal of the seventh Earl of Ravenholm. He had been the one who finished the tower, but he didn't make any note of the treasure. Perhaps he had never heard about it. But the previous two earls—his father and his brother—either didn't keep journals or they had been lost in time.

"Nothing in particular," she lied. "I should get you my journal."

Inspector Thayne frowned. "Journal?"

She nodded. "I copied everything into it that I've found out about this."

He stared at her before he chuckled softly and reached out to touch her hand again. "You're full of surprises."

"Yes, well…" she trailed off. In the hallway, she could hear Mr. Semple announce that it was time to dress for dinner. "I'll get it for you after dinner."

"Thank you."

With one last squeeze of her hand, he led her over to the others.

CHAPTER THIRTEEN

Thea wished she had given more thought to what she would wear to dinner that day. She didn't want to look frumpy next to Charlie, who had bought a whole new wardrobe. She didn't even want to think about what the other girls would wear. It made Thea long to go shopping, just so she could look her best the next three days for Inspector Thayne.

When she opened the door to her room, Bridget was inside. A package laid open on the bed. The wrapping paper held three different pairs of gloves, several hair ornaments, and an envelope. Bridget had unpacked the matching slips and petti-coats and laid them on the bed. The silks and laces shimmered in the light and Thea resisted the urge to reach out to run a hand over the garments.

"Please forgive me, my lady," the maid cried as she saw Thea. "I wasn't going to open it but I was dying of curiosity."

Hanging on the door of the wardrobe was one of the most beautiful dresses she had ever seen, until she saw the three beside it. The colors on each were deep, the exact shades of the jewels she had brought with her to Scotland. Only one person knew what jewelry she had brought with her. Not even Bridget would have seen it all.

"It's from Fletcher's," the maid continued, her words bordering on frantic, "and I've never been to a department store before. And then I saw it was a dress and I thought it should air out and…" She swallowed, taking a breath. "I brought the kitten back downstairs as soon as I saw the lace."

Thea nodded. "Thank you."

She swallowed, took a step closer to the bed, and popped the seal on the envelope.

Dear Lady Thea,

I said that you would be fine without me but I may have overesti-mated that I would be fine without you. After working for you all these years, I hope you don't find offense if I say I came to think of you as my family.

I know you were nervous about the party and that you have prob-ably invited the handsome Inspector Thayne to attend. The two of you made a wonderful team and I hope that your friendship with him will continue to flourish.

These dresses are from our new collection from a designer we are sampling. I know they are a bit flashier than you prefer but since I am no longer your maid, I can tell you that you needed a new wardrobe.

Your friend, Molly Talbot

P.S. I have included instructions for which dress to wear on each day and how to pair each with gloves, jewels, and undergarments. I'm sure your maid will find it helpful.

Thea grinned and passed the second piece of paper to Bridget. The maid's eyes widened as she took it in. "My lady?"

"Follow her instructions."

The maid stared at the page before she nodded. "Yes, my lady."

The gown that Molly had picked out for dinner that night was a cream-colored silk covered by a beaded, lacy overdress of emerald. Tiny jet beads decorated the sleeves and the neckline of the overdress. A cream sash with a diamond buckle accented the high waist.

There was no way that this was *prêt-à-porter*—ready to wear —as Molly claimed. Most women would never be able to afford such an elaborate gown, even if it was only a dinner dress.

Thea pulled out her jewelry box. Molly's notes told her to wear the strand of coral beads that could easily reach her knees and was long enough to wrap around her neck four times if she opened the golden clasp.

She would have to write Molly later and thank her for the beautiful gowns. She definitely needed to visit Fletcher's when she was back in London. Perhaps Charlie could come with her. Charlie would enjoy seeing so many beautiful clothes under one roof.

Bridget offered her the black gloves and fastened the feathered pin into Thea's hair. When she was done, the woman in the mirror was not entirely one Thea was familiar with. She looked like one of the drawings from a magazine or one of the house models in Paris.

She swept from the room, the train of the gown slithering on the floor behind her.

The guests had all gathered in the drawing room as they waited for dinner. Her aunt looked beautiful as always. Charlie was dressed in the gown she had spoken endlessly about on the ride to the castle. Most people wouldn't bat an eye at how she was dressed but when Thea walked into the room that night, it felt like all of the eyes were on her.

A grin threatened to split Inspector Thayne's face when he saw her. His steps were measured, like he had to stop himself from walking too fast across the room.

"You look lovely," he whispered as he offered her his arm.

"Thank you." She beamed at him, giggling softly, feeling more carefree than she had in a long time. Perhaps it had to do with the way he looked at her.

The walk into the dining room was relatively quiet. Thea found herself sitting between Inspector Thayne and James but the latter had barely said a word to her through the meal. He was polite but she felt as if they were suddenly two strangers who had never talked before.

"I'm sorry," she said softly. "I was cruel earlier."

James took a deep breath.

"You were right though," he said, and then quieter to himself, he added, "I haven't given you any reason to think I have your best interest at heart, have I?"

Something about that struck her as odd. Everything about him was odd, including the strange conversation they'd had when they had walked around the grounds of the castle.

"I still shouldn't have said it."

He glanced at her, his expression softening.

"Why do you care what happens to me anyway?" She tried to keep her tone light but inside, her mind was whirling. He had no reason to worry about her.

James opened his mouth to speak, just as the plates were replaced with dessert. The moment interrupted, he shook his head.

"We'll talk later."

Her brow furrowed, wondering why they couldn't talk then. What could he possibly have to say that he didn't want overheard by others?

She glanced back toward Inspector Thayne, who was picking at his dessert and staring blankly at Sylvia. The girl chattered at him but she didn't seem to realize that he was only paying attention to what Thea and James were saying. She'd have almost felt bad for the girl. Thea had spent many dinners being ignored by whichever male companion her host had seated her near. It didn't help that she felt like she never had anything interesting to say.

Across the table, Wilhelmina looked away from Anthony to watch them intensely.

The rest of the dinner passed in near silence between the three of them. It was uncomfortable. James had returned to small talk, mentioning the weather and the next day's hunting like those were the most exciting things that he could think of.

When they were freed to the drawing room, it was almost too soon.

The men separated to smoke their cigars and sip their brandy and do whatever it was they did when they were away from the women. Thea sat to play cards with the three other unmarried ladies and stayed quiet as they gossiped and giggled. Across the room, Wilhelmina sat with Great Aunt Mary and Lady Thayne. Wilhelmina was back to speaking in that over-exaggerated accent.

Lady Thayne looked lovely in her tiara and dark gray dress. She looked soft, approachable, and welcoming. Great Aunt Mary, on the other hand, was an intimidating older woman. As a countess who had outlasted her husband, she had to be but she was nowhere near as terrifying as Thea's grand-mother. She wasn't critical of Thea and didn't find fault in every little thing she did.

After the ordeal on the train, her grandmother had sent a telegram immediately, followed by a scathing eight-page letter detailing how it wasn't a lady's place to do such things. All from an article that was shorter than most of the headlines.

"You're doing terribly tonight," Charlie noted as Thea lost yet another hand.

"It's because she's madly in love, torn between two hand-some bachelors," Sylvia teased, batting her eyelashes and fanning herself with her cards.

Emma placed one of her cards across the table. "That's my cousin you're talking about. He's practically my brother."

Thea rolled her eyes. "I'm not madly in love with anyone."

"'The lady doth protest too much, methinks,'" was Sylvia's response.

Charlie picked up the cards from the table and reshuffled the deck.

Sylvia leaned in, looking directly at Charlie. "What do you think about Lady Thea's romances?"

Her cousin didn't hesitate or look up. Her hands never stopped moving as she dealt the cards. "I think she and Inspector Thayne make for a handsome couple."

Thea stared at the table helplessly. Give her a murderer any day. It was far better than dealing with girls who were trying to live vicariously through her and her non-existent romances.

"Oh!" Emma's soft voice came, "I think you might be right. She's turning rather red."

Thea glanced at them, standing up. "Well, this was fun."

"What? Where are you going?" Sylvia protested, as Emma's eyes started watering on command.

"It was all just in good fun."

"Really, Thea," Charlie mocked, frowning, "I'd have thought you'd know better by now."

"Please sit down," Emma begged, "We'll stop."

The other two girls nodded.

Thea huffed as she gave in, glancing at her cards. Another horrid hand.

THE NIGHT COULDN'T HAVE BEEN OVER FAST ENOUGH. As soon as she was able, Thea made her escape, taking the stairs as fast as she dared without appearing to run. Still, it wasn't fast enough.

"You're an idiot," a voice came from behind her as she reached the landing.

"Excuse me?" Thea turned to the American woman.

"The handsome Inspector and the brave reporter. I noticed what happened during dinner. You talked but then something happened to cause the three of you to ignore each other."

Thea glared, looking away. She had forgotten how observant Wilhelmina could be. Her act as a meek lady had Thea fooled. "Well at least I'm not a fraud."

"Excuse me?" Wilhelmina asked in a low, sibilant tone, "What's that supposed to mean?"

"I saw how you let your husband treat you. What happened to the woman from the train? That woman was fearless."

Her face shuddered. "You know nothing. My husband, he's…"

She trailed off, drawing back as footsteps approached on the stairs.

"I wondered where you got off to," Mr. Livingston said as he approached. Something about him made her stomach knot and Thea took a step back instinctively, shifting so she was almost next to the wall.

"I'm sorry to have worried you." Wilhelmina's tone and manner changed from moments before. Her eyes were vacant and her face lost its expression.

Mr. Livingston turned his gaze on Thea, and she fought not to swallow hard. "Please excuse my wife and me, Lady Theodora."

"Of course."

She forced a smile onto her face, moving completely out of their way as Wilhelmina's husband led Wilhelmina away.

"There's something odd about him, wouldn't you say?" Inspector Thayne asked as he came up the stairs.

"There is. Wilhelmina acts so strange around him."

He offered her his arm and they strolled along the corridor.

"I noticed that too." His eyes narrowed. "Please don't interfere in their affairs though. I'm sure there's a reason for their behavior."

Thea was sure there was too but she doubted it was anything good.

He didn't release her arm until they reached her door.

"As pleasant as this is, Inspector, you hardly need to escort me to my room. What would people think?"

He laughed softly. "Ah but there is a reason. An official police matter you promised you'd handle." Her face must have shown her confusion, because he shook his head fondly. "Your journal."

"Yes, of course." She reached for the doorknob. "I'll get that for you right away."

Her room had been straightened up since she left for dinner. Bridget must have put away the other gowns that Molly sent.

Thea pulled off her gloves, laying them haphazardly on the desk, not even noticing the kitten laying there until he lifted his head. The glove made for an odd hat on him. Bridget would be back any minute and Thea didn't want to start too much gossip about the handsome inspector standing outside her door.

Once she had the journal, she gathered her skirt so she wouldn't trip as she crossed the room hastily. Inspector Thayne waited amused outside the door.

She held the journal out to him but didn't let go. "I'll need it back when you're done with it."

"Of course, my lady." His fingers brushed hers as he took it, a shock running through her fingers.

He moved his hand to take hers, his skin warm against hers. Her mouth went dry as he raised her hand and pressed his lips against the bare skin of her knuckles.

"Good night, Lady Thea," he said softly as he reluctantly released her hand.

"Good night, Inspector."

He smiled at her before he turned and walked away.

If the door frame hadn't been next to her, she might have lost her balance. As it was, she was feeling a bit unsteady on her feet.

Of course, that was when Bridget approached, eyes wide.

"Not a word," she told Bridget as the maid closed the door behind them. The maid bowed her head, a knowing smile on her face. Even the kitten seemed to smirk at her after that.

CHAPTER FOURTEEN

THE NEXT MORNING, SOMETHING SOFT HIT HER NOSE, WAKING her abruptly from sleep. Yawning, Thea reached a hand up and brushed it away. A meow came next and it startled her more than it probably should have. She blinked several times, her eyes clearing just as his forehead knocked into her cheek.

"Meow," greeted the kitten, sticking his tongue out to lick her nose.

"Good morning." She scratched behind his ears. "I suppose you still need a name."

If she was being truthful, she hadn't really thought about a name for him in days. She probably should name him something before he wouldn't respond to anything.

She sat up and he darted away, taking her slipper under the bed with him.

"Are you serious?" she muttered as she climbed from the bed. Before she could bend down to look for the slipper, the kitten dropped her wristwatch on her pillow. Thea could clearly remember putting the watch inside the box on top of the vanity. He shouldn't have been able to get to it.

"You little thief. How'd you get that?" she muttered to him as he yawned, his tiny fang-like teeth flashing in the dim morning light. She took the watch, slipped it onto her wrist, and knelt to fish for her slipper. At first, she didn't find it but instead something cold and metal. She pulled it out.

Her pen.

Flattening herself to the floor, despite it not being the most ladylike thing to do, she reached under the bed again. This time, she found the slipper but she also found her trunk key, the missing silver star hairpin, several hair ribbons, and the set of gloves she had given the kitten. Thea pulled herself from the floor, glaring at the cat.

"You really are a thief, aren't you?"

He licked his paw innocently, ignoring her. Arrogant little creature.

"That's what I'll name you. Mercury, after the Roman god of thieves."

He purred loudly at that, so she supposed that meant he approved of the name. She picked him up, holding onto him tightly so he couldn't escape and steal anything else.

"Good morning, my lady." Bridget opened the curtains and let the sunshine in. Thea and Mercury both blinked as the light flooded the room and the kitten let out an unhappy meow in protest.

Thea grinned. "I found our ghost."

Bridget blinked as Thea motioned to the kitten. Mercury wailed loudly as if to proclaim his innocence.

"But he's just a baby," the maid murmured.

"He's been hiding everything under the bed. Perhaps today, we should find somewhere for him where he's less likely to take things. I don't want to bring him with me. The noise would be too much." Thea walked to the window and glanced at the sky. The sun shone brightly despite the clouds but it was clear that it was going to be perfect weather later. Not too hot but not too cold. "It's a beautiful day for a hunt."

"Of course, my lady." The look she got from Bridget told her the maid didn't believe that either of those things was really the reason for Thea's high spirits. "I can make a bed for him in the bath. There's nothing in there that he should be able to hurt himself on but he shouldn't be able to hide anything either."

Thea nodded and passed Mercury to her. "Thank you."

BREAKFAST CONSISTED OF THE SAME FOODS AS ALWAYS BUT since there were more people than usual, getting to the sideboard became something of a dance. She was thankful for the shorter hem of her day dress. On a previous occasion, her heel had caught on the back of her dress and she spilled her plate over a marquess. This year, as she started to stumble, she felt a hand on her back, steadying her.

"Easy," a voice murmured in her ear. She turned her head slightly as she regained her footing. James stood behind her, supporting her.

She stared at him and he jerked his hand away like she had burned him.

"Are you all right?" Anthony asked as he passed them.

"I'm fine." Thea plastered a smile on her face as she gripped her plate tighter and headed over to the table.

James sat down next to her at the table, though after the way they'd left things between them the night before, she was surprised he'd want to. It didn't help that he kept dismissing her question with the same three words: "We'll talk later."

Later had come and gone many times over. She never took him for a coward.

"Are you going on the hunt today?" James asked as he passed her the marmalade.

Thea shook her head. "I hadn't given it any thought either way."

"Would you accompany me?"

She paused her movements. He met her eyes briefly and she swallowed. "All right."

James looked back to his food, nodding.

Inspector Thayne entered the room, followed by Inspector Anderson. The former looked at her until a blush overtook her face. She thought he might sit next to her but Josiah Thayne stole the seat beside her. His brother's expression soured a little.

"So," the young Scottish lord-to-be started, "what's going on between you and my brother?"

Thea stared at him and she heard James chuckle.

"Haven't you heard?" the reporter drawled.

Josiah's eyes flickered to him. "Heard?"

"Lady Theodora and your brother are in a vicious cycle of him telling her to stay away from police investigations and her not listening."

Josiah laughed, glancing across the table at his brother. Thea glared at James, who merely shrugged his shoulders.

"I'd hardly say that," Thea defended, fighting to not cross her arms over her chest, "It's not a vicious cycle."

"Let's agree to disagree."

THE CRISP MORNING AIR BROUGHT THICK CLOUDS OF FOG THAT hung low over the horizon. The briskness of the morning made her shiver. Thea hoped that it wouldn't stay that way once the sun came up fully and warmed the fields and forest, otherwise the hunt might be more dangerous than planned.

Thea wore a tweed suit, the same as the others on the hunt.

Most of the ladies would join at the midday luncheon but Lady Thayne had also opted to go with the men, which Thea found surprising.

"Have you ever been out during one of the hunts?" Lady Thayne asked her as she approached. A shotgun was bent over her arm. One of the dogs nipped at her feet.

"No but I'm looking forward to it."

The woman smiled at her. "You're in for a treat."

"Are you shooting then?"

"I always do."

Thea blinked, staring at her. She had heard of women going on hunts and a few participating but she had never actually seen it.

"I'll watch for you," Thea promised.

With that, the baroness strode back over towards her husband. Inspector Thayne loaded his shotgun beside Anthony. They talked about something that seemed to agitate the inspector.

"Are you ready?" James asked as he trudged through the dewy grass, shotgun slung over the crook of his arm. One of Uncle Malcolm's spaniels sat proudly beside him, seemingly unaware that the grass was wet.

"I suppose I have to be."

"I'm hardly dragging you out here. There's plenty of time to turn back." She stared at him. He didn't know her as well as he thought if he believed she'd leave then.

She shrugged. "Might as well see what all the fuss is about."

He shook his head and laughed quietly.

They wandered through the wet, muddy ground. The air was damp enough that she was surprised the midges weren't out yet. Usually Thea found herself covered in bites when she wandered outside. But it had been unseasonably cold for most of her trip, when usually it got colder not long before she left.

"Ready," James said gently as he stopped, taking aim far enough away from the others that they were out of earshot but not out of sight.

Instinctively, she lifted her hands to cover her ears. The noise was still far louder than she expected and she jumped. The spaniel took off after whatever it was James had shot.

"We should talk."

"You keep saying that but we haven't."

James ducked his head, checking his ammunition. It probably wasn't wise to anger him while he held the shotgun. But he didn't seem cross at her statement, only a bit sheepish. His cheeks were flush but she wondered if that wasn't from the cold.

"Only because I'm not sure how to say this." He glanced up at her for a second, meeting her eyes for the first time since they had walked out during the hunt.

Thea watched him as he shoved another shell into the barrel. "Don't think. Just say whatever it is."

He looked at her.

"I'm your brother."

Thea froze, turning to stare at him, mouth open. Of all the things she expected him to say, that never crossed her mind.

That was, of course, when the dog came back with one of the ugliest birds Thea had ever seen. As he dropped the creature at their feet, she could have sworn the dog grinned at her.

She shook her head, trying to clear it. "How is that possible?"

"The woman I was talking about yesterday, my birth mother, is your mother."

Thea blinked. In retrospect, it felt a little like she should have realized it. It made sense and it explained why James cared about what happened to her.

"Huh," was about the only response she could formulate.

"Are you angry?" His tone was soft but she could hear the tension behind his words.

"Why?" she asked as they started walking again. "What would be the point in being angry at you?"

"I didn't tell you on the train. Aren't you mad that I waited?"

"You didn't know me. I didn't know you." She wrung her hands together as she studied him. "Do you want me to be angry with you?"

He smiled nervously. "Not particularly."

"Why were you on the train anyway? Were you looking for me?"

James laughed, and it sounded as shaky as she felt. He shook his head. "It was pure coincidence. I was going to let you and your brother live in peace."

She didn't know why that made her heart clench painfully.

"But then, there you were in the dining car, eating by yourself, and you just looked so… miserable and scared and overwhelmed. I didn't want to leave you like that. I had to help."

She watched him as he spoke. She could see it now that she knew to look for it. He didn't have her mother's eyes or hair but the nose was the same, as was the way he smiled. She didn't know how she had ever missed it.

"And then it was just so easy, talking to you, teasing you. I felt like I had known you my whole life."

One question nagged at the front of her mind more than the others.

"Would you have ever told me?"

He hesitated and she had her answer. The fact that he wouldn't have told her shouldn't have stung the way it did. She turned and started to head back to the rest of the hunting party.

"Thea," he said, calling her by her chosen name for the first time since she'd met him. He had been so steadfast in calling her Theodora. That, more than anything, made her pause.

"I almost did. Six years ago. You were all supposed to be here. Your father arranged it. When you weren't here, it felt like a sign that it wasn't meant to happen. But if I had known when your father first approached me what I know now, I wouldn't have stayed away."

His words didn't remove the sting of how many years had passed since he'd found out about Cecil and her and he had never chosen to make contact with them.

She wasn't even going to think about her mother. How could she have lied to them for all these years?

It was strange to think that she had another brother who had lived a whole life away from their family. She wished she had been able to know him when they were younger but she was happy that they had found each other.

"Who's your father?"

He shook his head. "That's rather complicated."

She rolled her eyes. "You're my illegitimate half-brother. It can hardly be more complicated. Not unless Uncle Malcolm's really your father." She paused at the thought. "He's not though, is he?"

James laughed and shook his head again. "No, he's not. Do you remember Colonel Bantry from the train?"

She stared at him, eyes wide. "Are you serious?"

"Yes." He looked a bit bewildered by her reaction.

"He's my favorite author." She shook her head. "He's really your father?"

"Yes." He glanced back towards the rest of the party.

In retrospect, it wasn't that difficult to see the familiar resemblance between him and the Colonel. Now, some of James' actions on the train made more sense.

"I met him when I was in India."

Thea looked over to him. "Why were you in India?"

"For work, of course."

Across the field, Lady Thayne took aim and fired. Despite knowing that the baroness planned to hunt, Thea was surprised to see it.

"Do you know how to shoot?" he asked. Thea shook her head. Her parents had never let her go out on the hunts. Her aunt and uncle were always reluctant when she was a child. This visit, everyone had been handling her with kid gloves. She was tired of it. "Would you like to?"

Thea swallowed and held out her hand.

James helped her position the gun against her shoulder, guiding her left hand beneath the barrel. She was surprised by how heavy it was and started to lean back on instinct.

"Spread your feet and lean forward a little." She did. "Bring your cheek down." Thea looked up, staring at him. He was joking, right? "If you don't, it'll hit you in the face when you fire. And you need to look down the barrel to aim."

She did as he said, letting him aim her towards one of the grouse. When she squeezed the trigger, it was perhaps one of the loudest sounds she had ever heard in her life. The gun jerked into her shoulder and cheek but not nearly as badly as it could have.

She handed the gun back to James as the dog came back with the bird. Everything ached but she was unable to wipe the grin off of her face. No wonder Lady Thayne hunted.

"Not bad for your first time," he murmured as Anthony came towards them.

"I can't believe you actually did that," her cousin exclaimed.

To be fair, she couldn't either.

Anthony glanced back at the others. "We're heading over for lunch."

As they rejoined the group, Lady Thayne favored her with a smile. "That was an admirable shot for your first time."

"Thank you."

"Quite a way to end the morning. We'll have to have you to Hollindale Abbey sometime, won't we, darling?"

Lord Thayne blinked when he realized his wife was talking to him. "Of course."

CHAPTER FIFTEEN

THE LUNCHEON WAS LAID OUT UNDER A LARGE CANOPY. A TABLE covered with a white tablecloth was set up with wicker chairs surrounding it and a view of the loch. The water looked particularly blue that day and the gray clouds of early that morning had dissipated.

The rest of the women waited for them. They wore various shades of tweed suits but were much cleaner than Thea's mud-soaked hem and muck-covered boots. But Lady Thayne's clothes were also soiled.

Thea took her seat and was glad that she had a pleasant view of the water.

"I take it you and Mr. Poyntz worked things out between the two of you," Inspector Thayne said as he sat down beside her. Normally, she would have been annoyed at her aunt's blatant attempts to set her up with the inspector but in this case, Thea didn't mind it so much. He was actually someone she wanted to be around.

"We did but I'll tell you about it later." Thea didn't want to keep it a secret from the inspector but she didn't want the others overhearing while she and James were still figuring out things between them.

"Perhaps you'd like to accompany me when we go back out?"

Thea grinned at him. "I would love to."

Francis Livingston took the seat on the other side of her, smirking as he did. There was something about him that made her want to shy away. He leered at her, and Thea leaned away from him. "My dear Lady Thea, perhaps you'd rather accompany me."

A shadow passed over the man's face as James stopped beside them.

"The lady didn't give you permission to be so familiar with her," he said. Francis jumped to his feet.

"What would you know about anything, you middle class—?"

"Gentlemen, enough." Inspector Anderson stepped between them before it could come to blows.

James glared at the younger Livingston brother before he continued to his place next to Charlie. The others watched with interest but as soon as everyone was seated, they pretended like they hadn't seen a thing.

"I saw you shooting earlier," the inspector said softly to her, low enough to keep the conversation between them.

"Mr. Poyntz is a rather good instructor."

Something flashed in Inspector Thayne's eyes. "Yes, I imagine so."

She glanced around and noticed that Emma had leaned in closer to eavesdrop. "I'll tell you about it after lunch."

Inspector Thayne glanced behind him. Emma straightened and plastered an innocent expression on her face. Thea frowned. If she said anything more, she knew that Emma would wind up passing what she heard to Charlie and Sylvia. She'd never hear the end of it.

"Personally, I'd love to know more." The girl smiled from the other side of Inspector Thayne.

Thea rolled her eyes and sat back.

"Are you enjoying yourself so far, Miss Poyntz?" Thea asked over the Inspector, despite the fact that it was rather rude to do so. She was hoping that the girl would get her hint to leave the conversation alone.

"Oh, it's been lovely. But I think I'd much rather accompany the rest of you on the hunt after lunch. I don't want to miss all the excitement."

Emma fixed them both with a dazzling grin. For a moment, Thea wished she was as charming as the girl but she suspected it didn't matter to Inspector Thayne. His was really the only opinion that mattered to her.

The meal finished and the others left the table. The men collected their shotguns. The ladies mostly gathered on the far side of the canopy. Their voices carried as the women planned what they should do next and the girls giggled. Inspector Thayne and Anthony seemed to be talking about something and Thea stood to join them.

Francis grabbed her wrist. His grip tightened, nails digging into her skin. She yelped and tried to yank her arm away.

"Let go of me!" she ordered.

"Not until you agree to accompany me, *Lady Thea*," he sneered her name, making it sound like a curse.

"Never, you pig." With her free hand, she slapped him hard enough to make his head jerk in the other direction. Unfortunately, it didn't have the desired effect and he gripped her arm tight enough for her to cry out.

"You little—"

Thea didn't know when James had come around, only that the younger Livingston was on the ground, clutching his nose.

Inspector Thayne grabbed James by the arms and hauled

him back before he could land another punch. Inspector Anderson held Francis back.

"Let me see it," she vaguely heard Anderson say to Livingston over the sound of buzzing in her ears but she had turned away, unable to stand the sight of him any longer. The others had gone silent.

James appeared to have calmed down so Inspector Thayne let him go.

"Did he hurt you?" her brother asked but the inspector was at his heels.

She pulled the glove off slowly. Her wrist was red but the leather of the glove seemed to have protected her from most of it. For that at least, she was grateful.

"I'm fine," she breathed. "You didn't have to hit him."

James stared, before he snorted. "Yes, I did." He glanced over at Inspector Thayne. "Although, I'm surprised I beat you to it, Inspector."

"I'm more surprised that I stopped you," he muttered, almost too low for any of them to hear.

"Well, I appreciate it."

"With as much trouble as you get into, perhaps you ought to learn Ju-Jitsu like those suffragettes."

"I thought the idea was for Lady Thea to stay out of trouble, Mr. Poyntz, not for her to learn to fight."

James laughed but it was bitter. "I'm under no impression that she's able to stay out of trouble. I'd rather she knows how to get out of it."

"I'd rather know too," Thea agreed, "And I'd appreciate you both not talking about me like I'm not standing in front of you."

Inspector Thayne flushed. James glanced down, looking a little like a chastised schoolboy.

"What's going on over here?" Inspector Anderson looked between the three of them. "Are you all right, my lady?"

She smiled and nodded. "Yes. Thank you, Inspector."

"Mr. Livingston doesn't wish to press charges, Mr. Poyntz. He wouldn't tell me what happened to provoke you in the first place. Would you care to share why you hit him?"

James looked up, defiance in his eyes but Inspector Thayne stepped in and spoke. "Mr. Livingston had a hold on Lady Thea and refused to release her when she asked."

James grabbed her arm much more gently than Livingston had, displaying the reddened skin for the older inspector to see.

"Had a hold on her is putting it mildly," her brother snarled at both of the policemen. Anderson's eyes narrowed as he took in her wrist.

"I see. My lady, would you care to press charges?"

Thea shook her head. She doubted the man would try anything with her again. He'd probably worry that he'd end up with more than a broken nose.

She was unusually aware of everyone watching them. James stalked off to get his gun but Thea stayed with Inspector Thayne.

Maybe the younger Livingston was the one who killed Kate all those years ago. It made sense in a sick sort of way. If Livingston had the nerve to try that with Thea, he'd have no problem trying such a thing with a maid.

Even if he hadn't killed Kate, Thea didn't want to venture too close to the younger Mr. Livingston again, just in case.

THE LADIES JOINED THE HUNT AFTER LUNCH, MOSTLY TO spectate. The thing that they seemed to find the most fascinating was the idea of Lady Thayne hunting but Thea wondered if they were using that as an excuse to watch for the next fight between the men. From the way they kept looking in her direction, Thea was sure that most of their conversation was about her.

Away from the others, Inspector Thayne lined up his sight on a bird and took a shot. His dog, one of the ones his family had brought, ran out to fetch it. He had refused to make eye contact with her since they'd walked over and Thea hated that it felt like she was starting the morning all over again with a different person.

"Mr. Poyntz is rather defensive of you," he said, staring off in the direction his dog had gone. His tone was dark and she fought the urge to flinch back. She didn't believe that the inspector would ever harm her but the way he spoke felt like a frigid winter.

"He finally told me why this morning." At this, Inspector Thayne turned sharply to stare at her. "He's my brother."

"What?" The anger had drained from his voice, his words more shocked that anything.

"I guess really he's my half-brother. At least, that's what he said."

"You doubt him then?"

"No." She shook her head, letting out a sigh. "I just wish I knew why my mother never told me. And James said he met my father before he died but he never said anything either."

"Perhaps they were trying to protect you?" the inspector reasoned. "Or protect themselves."

That seemed likely. Her father loved her mother. It made sense that he'd keep her secrets for her. But her mother, Thea wished she understood why she had kept it from Cecil and her. Was she ashamed of her pre-marital indiscretion? That would make the most sense.

Thea's American grandparents were both rather strict. Her uncle hadn't rebelled against them but her aunt had. Her aunt Dorothea raced motorcars on the circuits of the rich and famous, and died young. She left her fortune to Thea with the explanation that she didn't want Thea to be beholden to anyone.

It only made sense that her mother had rebelled as well. She remembered what Colonel Bantry said on the train, about a whirlwind affair that had ended with her mother married and the Colonel joining the army to travel to India. Knowing what she did now, everything the Colonel said about his once-mysterious love and her family made sense.

Thea shook her head to clear it.

"I kept thinking that there was something so familiar about James that I just couldn't put my finger on. It crossed my mind every time I saw him."

Inspector Thayne chuckled as he lowered the shotgun again, sounding rather like a weight had been taken off his shoulders.

"I, for one, am glad to know Mr. Poyntz's true identity." Her eyebrows furrowed as she glanced at him. "I can't very well be jealous of your brother, now can I?"

"Jealous, Inspector?" Thea asked. "Whatever are you jealous about?"

He took a step towards her. "I'm jealous that other people get to spend more time around you than I do. And that he was able to be there for you when you needed help on the train." Another step, so that he was close enough that the toes of their boots touched. Her head tilted back slightly so that she could look him in the eye. "And that, when I arrived, you were walking in with him and I had no way of knowing what had gone on between you."

"You don't need to be jealous, Inspector."

"You know, you could call me Leslie," he muttered softly, a breath's width away. His hand stroked her gloved one. Her heart felt like it might explode from her chest.

"But that wouldn't be acceptable," she whispered, trying her best for coy, "Especially not in public."

"We're not in public right now."

"Leslie," she breathed, leaning in until all she could smell was his cologne.

A shot rang through the air. That alone wouldn't have fazed her if a bloodcurdling scream hadn't followed it.

They jumped apart, the moment broken.

Leslie turned back towards the group. Thea looked over his shoulder and saw the others gathering around something. The ladies mostly stayed back but the men leaned over whatever it was.

"We should go see what happened," she said, without really meaning it. She wanted to fall back into that moment but it was over.

Together, they trudged through the field. Wilhelmina's eyes were wide and terrified as they approached. She turned until she met Thea's but she shook her head before Thea could come any closer to the women. So instead, she pinned herself to Leslie's side.

"What happened?" Leslie asked James, who shook his head, his shotgun slung over his arm. His face was pale and his hands seemed to shake. She wasn't the only one who noticed that though. The others were giving him cautious looks.

"I didn't shoot him," her brother said low enough that only they could hear, his words delivered like he was giving a report, unemotional and uninvested, a stark contrast to his otherwise unsteadiness. "I was facing south. He was the other direction."

"Shoot who?" Leslie prodded.

James motioned the inspector forward but he reached out, taking Thea by the elbow. Whatever was on the ground, he didn't want her to see.

Still, she looked.

Francis Livingston laid on the ground, completely still, blood running from the hole in his chest.

CHAPTER SIXTEEN

EVERYTHING SEEMED TO MOVE RATHER QUICKLY AFTER THAT. Inspector Anderson positioned himself between the guests and the body. Leslie stepped forward to get a better look and the Edinburgh inspector let him, the two men discussing something in hushed tones.

"Let me go," Thea muttered to her brother, who still had a hold on her elbow, keeping her from wandering too close to the scene.

"You don't honestly think I did it?" Hurt filled James' eyes.

"No but I want a look." He didn't let go or relax his grip, only shifting to place himself between her and the body.

"Did you happen to go to medical school and I don't know about it?" he asked, a bit snide. "Because that's the only way I'm letting you examine a body in front of the police."

Thea frowned. "Now I wish I had."

The truth was that she didn't have any formal education past what most of the other girls her age were given. With all the murders happening around her, she thought it would be nice to have had some extra knowledge to aid her.

He scoffed, as if he knew what she was thinking. "Like I said earlier, you and trouble."

"I'm not the one that everyone thinks shot a man." At least, she assumed that was what they thought from the wary glances the others kept giving James.

His expression darkened but his tone stayed even. "I didn't kill him."

"I'm not saying you did. But someone did."

"Why didn't they do that this morning? It was foggy then. It would have been easier to pass it off as an accident."

She shrugged, hoping she came across calmer than she felt. "Everyone saw you fight at lunch. As far as they're concerned, you hit him for no reason."

"There was every reason," James growled. "I feel like I'm talking to a wall with you sometimes." She shook her head. "Why is it so odd that I can't stand back when you're in trouble?"

His words touched her. To be honest, Cecil had never seemed to feel that way. When Cecil's inebriated friend had put his hands on her years ago, Cecil thought that Thea was interested in that lout. As much as she loved her younger brother, he wasn't the most observant and had never jumped to her rescue the way James did.

Perhaps he was overcompensating for the years he had chosen to stay away. But his protectiveness didn't scare her. In fact, it made her feel rather invincible.

Leslie stepped away from the body and ushered everyone back.

"Listen up!" He told the crowd. "We're heading inside and everyone is going to stay together until the local police can conduct their investigation."

"But it was just an accident, wasn't it?" Anthony asked, his eyes hard as he stared directly at James.

"Don't be naïve," Mrs. Erskine chided. "We all saw the way *he* went after poor Mr. Livingston at lunch."

James crossed his arms, his jaw clenched but he didn't speak to defend himself. He seemed to know it would do no good.

Thea clenched her fist. She hated feeling so helpless but there really wasn't anything she could do at the moment. Everyone thought she was madly in love with James and nothing she said would help his case.

"It makes sense," Mr. Livingston said suddenly. "The way he clings to Lady Theodora, the minute my poor brother showed the slightest bit of affection towards her—"

It seemed that James had inherited their mother's temper. She saw the fire in his eyes as he started to move. Thea barely had a chance to grab his arm to keep him from lunging forward.

"Look!" Livingston declared, "Just an uncaged animal."

"Now really," Aunt Diana said, the voice of reason, "we don't know what happened—"

"We know exactly what happened. That man killed my brother."

The crowd went silent. No one wanted to vocalize that they thought James had killed the man, even if they were willing to imply it.

Wilhelmina took a step back, as if she was trying to hide herself from the crowd, or perhaps just her husband.

"He terrified my poor wife." Livingston grabbed Wilhelmina in a way that had to hurt.

"Mr. Livingston," Leslie interrupted again, "if you would please, we can continue in the house."

The man glared at him but gave a stiff, jerky nod.

The walk to the house was uncomfortable at best. Every time someone opened their mouth to speak, Leslie turned to shoot a glare in their direction. The heavy layers of tweed suddenly were stifling and Thea longed for nothing more than to change. She felt so dirty, though she couldn't entirely put into words as to why.

They gathered in the drawing room. Leslie left to contact the police but not before he warned them not to leave the room. Everyone was tense and no one really seemed to want to get too close to James. Emma had taken a spot on the couch with Sylvia and Charlie. James' aunt sat in the chair by Mrs. Erskine and Aunt Diana. His uncle stood with Uncle Malcolm, Mr. Erskine, and Lord Thayne by the fireplace.

"I suppose you'll be canceling the ball," Mrs. Erskine said to Aunt Diana like it was the most important thing at the moment. "It's awfully last minute but it just doesn't seem right."

"You shouldn't," Mr. Livingston's voice came, drawing all of the eyes in the room to him. "The ball was Francis' favorite part of this. He would have been upset to have it canceled because of him."

Something about that statement seemed so callous, so cold, despite the man's attempt to deliver it with feeling.

Her aunt nodded slowly, staring at him as if she didn't understand. "If you insist, Mr. Livingston…"

"I do."

For someone whose brother was just killed, Ernest Livingston seemed rather unaffected by the whole affair. If it was her brother who had been killed, she would have been upset. She would have been angry. Other than his short outburst outside, he was relatively quiet.

The younger Mr. Livingston had been a detestable human being, and the world was probably a better place without him but it was odd that his brother didn't seem to care. Thea might have suspected that Francis had killed Kate but she had no actual evidence that he did. With him dead, it was possible she'd never know.

But, what if he hadn't killed her? What if he knew who did? With her body so recently discovered, he would have been a liability. But if he knew, why wouldn't he have told the police?

She needed to get into his room before it was cleared or locked. With her luck, Inspector Anderson might decide that it should be treated as evidence and then she'd never get a look inside. But the key to why he was murdered might be in there.

As if she had heard Thea's thoughts, Bridget appeared, carrying a tray of tea. Two footmen followed with other refreshments.

"My lady," Bridget's voice came softly as she handed her a cup and saucer with the tea. "What happened?"

"The younger Mr. Livingston was shot during the hunt."

Her eyes went wide. "Is he going to be all right, my lady?"

Thea swallowed. "He's dead." She glanced over at her brother, currently staring into his teacup like it might hold some answers.

The maid inhaled sharply.

"Can you take a look in Mr. Livingston's room?" Thea whispered to her. Despite the fact that Leslie didn't trust Bridget, she needed the girl to be her eyes and ears in that room. They were supposed to stay in the drawing room but Leslie had never said anything about the servants leaving. She could only hope her trust wasn't misplaced. "Both Mr. Livingstons' rooms."

"Of course, my lady. Am I looking for something in particular?"

"Just any reason why someone would kill him."

Bridget swallowed.

"And hurry," Thea added, "before the police send someone to lock the room."

"Yes, my lady." She scurried from the room, as inconspicuously as she could. Not that any of the guests would actually pay attention to Bridget. Her maid's uniform made her practically invisible.

"What are you doing?" James asked as he joined her, looking rather amused.

"Nothing." He raised his brow at her. "Bridget's rather good at finding things out around the house. Especially things people don't want others to know."

"So you sent her to snoop." He snorted. "Of course."

"I can't sit around and do nothing. But unfortunately, that's all we're allowed to do."

"Welcome to civilian life, Theodora."

"I'm being serious."

"So am I." His jaw was set. "You're not trained for this. I don't want you getting hurt just because you're trying to prove that I didn't do something."

She crossed her arms, feeling a bit defensive. "I'm not doing it just for that. I'm also trying to find Kate's killer."

His expression darkened. "You think they're related."

"You don't?" she asked, surprise coloring her words. It seemed like the obvious conclusion.

He shook his head. "It could be a coincidence. But two murders occurring when the same group of guests are at the same house, it's unlikely."

She nodded.

Leslie came back into the room, only to be swarmed by the crowd of people, all desperate to know what was going to happen next. He fended them off with grace.

"Were you the closest to Mr. Livingston when it happened?" Thea asked as she listened to some of the ridiculous things the others were saying. None of the women, except for Lady Thayne, would have been able to shoot the man since none of them had a gun. But their husbands could have.

James gave her an odd look. "No. But that hardly clears my name."

"Someone had to have seen something," Thea insisted but James shook his head.

"It was chaotic enough that almost anyone could have done it." He eyed her for a moment. "Except you or the Inspector. You both looked rather… cozy."

She ducked her head, hoping to hide the blush she could feel rushing to her face.

"We weren't—"

"Spare me the lie." She glanced up at him. "Anyone with working eyes could see that the two of you fancy each other."

A smile crossed his face for a brief moment.

"Trouble," he muttered fondly. "Just… be careful, okay?"

She nodded. "I will."

He scrunched his nose. "And as much as it pains me to say it, I think Inspector Thayne is a good man. You can trust him."

Leslie fought his way free of the crowd and over to them. His eyes locked on Thea, an unreadable expression on his face. "Why did I see your maid heading up the stairs?"

She tried to plaster on an innocent expression. "Maybe she's checking on the kitten? Changing the bedclothes? Tidying the rooms?"

"And would one of the rooms she happened to be tidying be the late Mr. Livingston's?" Thea kept silent, even as James, the traitor, turned to her with an amused expression and raised eyebrow. "I see."

With a grin, James glanced at Leslie. "I told you earlier, Inspector, she loves trouble."

CHAPTER SEVENTEEN

"Lady Thea's already been cleared," Leslie explained to her aunt and uncle in a low voice.

Her aunt glared at the inspector and he shifted like a child caught doing something wrong. "But why her and no one else?"

"She has an alibi for the shooting."

"And the rest of us don't?" Uncle Malcolm said and Thea winced. She recognized the scathing tone that Uncle Malcolm used. "Exactly how long do we have to stay here?"

"The police will be here soon. They'll interview you and we'll be free to continue with the weekend." Leslie offered up a smile but Thea had a feeling it didn't actually help much.

He seemed unconcerned as he led her from the drawing room.

"Do you know which room was his?" he asked as they climbed the stairs and headed towards the guest wing.

"I think so."

She quickened her pace, hoping they wouldn't be too late to find Bridget before anyone else did.

"—thieves like you," Thea heard as they got closer to the late Mr. Livingston's room.

"I'm not a thief!"

"Sure, and I'm the Prince of Wales," Inspector Anderson's voice replied.

Dread settled in her stomach as she walked faster. As they turned the corner, they found Bridget standing in the corridor, being handcuffed by Inspector Anderson. The man glanced in their direction as they approached.

"I found her snooping around Mr. Livingston's room," Anderson told Leslie, practically ignoring Thea's presence. "The man's body is not even cold and his things are already being looted."

Leslie shot a quick glare at Thea. She bit her lip.

"I'm afraid that was my fault, Inspector," Leslie said. Thea jumped. Why would he take the blame for her mistake? "I didn't make myself clear when I told her to guard the room."

Bridget's eyes met Thea's, questioning but she kept silent.

"I see." He looked back at Bridget. "So why were you inside the room?"

The maid dropped her eyes, shifting guiltily. "I forgot to straighten up this morning. I didn't want Mrs. Campbell to find out. She'd fire me."

The inspector made a noise of disbelief but fortunately, Leslie stepped forward before the other man could begin questioning Bridget again.

"Since we're both here, why don't we take a look around the room?"

Anderson motioned towards the door. "Be my guest."

Leslie glanced at the handcuffs and Anderson reluctantly removed them from the maid. The girl practically flew to Thea's side.

"Lady Thea, why don't you both head to your room?"

Leslie phrased his words like a suggestion but Thea could feel the command behind them.

"Of course, Inspector Thayne." She glanced at her maid. "Come along, Bridget."

"Yes, my lady," the girl answered meekly.

Safely inside Thea's room, Bridget's expression crumpled. Her eyes shone brightly. It was the first time Thea had truly seen the girl lose her composure since Thea had been there.

"I'm sorry, my lady. I didn't mean to get caught."

"It's all right."

Bridget shook her head.

"He had all sorts of nasty letters but the Inspector caught me before I could grab them. But they're not true." The maid's breathing bordered on hysterical. Her hands trembled. "I'm glad he's dead. I'm glad he can't spread any more of those disgusting lies."

Bridget buried her face into her hands. Thea wrapped her arm around the girl and guided her to the chair to sit down.

"It's going to be fine. You'll see."

The girl swallowed hard as she nodded. "I hope so, my lady."

A loud wail echoed through the room that sounded a little like a child crying. Both Bridget and Thea jumped, glancing at each other.

"Mercury!" She moved through to the bath to check on the kitten. She was lucky to have one of the few rooms that had a mostly private bathroom that she shared with the other bedroom that connected to it.

To her surprise—though, perhaps it should haven't been a surprise—Mercury stood on top of the sink rather than in the bathtub where she had left him that morning. Considering the bathtub had a fluffy pillow, blankets, and plenty of fresh cream, she wasn't sure why he would have wanted to leave.

"Raaaooow!" he wailed as he saw her, as if to admonish

her for leaving him in such a sparse and boring room. She supposed that there lacked anything silver or shiny to steal—silver did seem to be his preference if the hairpin and Bridget's locket were any indication—even if they had left him with the gloves to play with.

"I'm sorry," she told him.

She reached out for him and he hissed, baring his tiny fangs at her. She flinched back out of reflex. Any time that little demon Arnold, her grandmother's cat, made that sound, it was better to be far away from him. But Mercury didn't seem like he was preparing to strike.

"I'm sorry," she whispered again.

This time, he let her come closer and meowed softly.

"It was better that you weren't there," she told him as she picked him up. "It was very loud and someone died."

"Meow?"

She scratched behind his ear and he settled into her arms as she took him back into her room.

It was only about a half hour before a knock sounded loudly on the door. Bridget was in no shape to answer, so Thea opened it herself to reveal Leslie.

"How is she?"

Thea shifted to the side so he was able to see the crying girl slumped in the chair. Mercury had settled himself at Bridget's feet and Thea hoped that gave Bridget some level of comfort.

"She's not in any trouble," Leslie said loud enough that Bridget heard, judging by the way her breathing hitched.

"Did he have anything?"

"There were some rather interesting blackmail letters that Francis Livingston wrote anonymously. He didn't use names but from what was written, the letters were clearly to multiple people."

Blackmail? That fit with Bridget's words about 'disgusting lies.'

"Bridget?" Thea asked as she glanced back at the maid. "Was Livingston blackmailing you?"

She glanced up, eyes wide with terror, and shook her head.

"Someone you know?" Leslie asked. At this, she nodded. "Who?"

"My father," the girl whimpered. "The letters threatened to have him fired. We never knew who sent them but then I saw the letters in his room…"

Thea blinked. She hadn't known that Bridget had family there. "Fired? Whatever for?"

Her maid swallowed hard. "Before we came here, he had trouble finding work. We did what we had to to survive. Lord Ravenholm was very kind giving us a chance." Bridget clenched her fists. "But that horrible man had all sorts of lies in his letters. He was going to tell Lord Ravenholm that we were stealing from him. But we weren't, my lady, I swear it. I haven't stolen a thing since we came here."

She was almost hysterical again. They both stared at her. The kitten wailed, jumping into Bridget's lap like he thought it would help her somehow.

To be fair, Thea had suspected that Bridget's past had been something like that since Bridget had come into her room with the ledgers. How else could she get such a thing from a locked room?

Leslie crossed his arms. "Who is your father?"

"Mr. Semple," the girl replied simply.

"Mr. Semple is your father?" Thea felt foolish that she hadn't known that already.

"Yes, my lady."

"Mr. Semple?" Leslie stared at her, his brow furrowing. "Isn't that the butler's name?"

Thea nodded.

"Huh." It felt like an appropriate summation of the conversation.

Mr. Semple had been at Ravenholm for ages. He had always been so kind and proper. To blackmail him for things that happened years ago wasn't right.

"Well, Inspector Anderson and Constable Mitchell have currently determined Mr. Livingston's death as an accident, regardless of the fact that there were those letters." Leslie frowned and she thought it was pretty clear that he didn't think it was an accident.

"You don't believe James did it, do you?" she asked. At the moment, he seemed like the most obvious choice.

Leslie shook his head. "He may have a temper but he's hardly the type to shoot someone in the back after the fact."

At least one of the policemen in the castle could see sense.

"They also determined that Mr. Livingston was the one to kill Kate." Doubt flickered over his face.

"But—" Bridget said, her voice cutting off as she looked down.

Thea turned back to her. "What is it?"

The maid pulled a crumpled letter out of the pocket of her apron. "I found this in his room, right before Inspector Anderson found me."

Thea blinked, walking forward to take the letter. She unfolded it carefully, smoothing out the creases. Ink splotches dotted the page and several words were crossed out, as if it was just a draft.

"It's dated yesterday. 'I know what you did to the maid,'" Thea read aloud. Leslie inhaled sharply. "'You shoved her into the wall. She fought back and you killed her. The deadline approaches. If you don't want anyone else to find out, deliver five hundred pounds to the east garden, under the statue of the angel, at 9 tomorrow.'"

"Livingston didn't kill her then," Leslie breathed. "The maid, I mean."

Thea nodded slowly, passing him the letter. "He was blackmailing the killer."

"He was incredibly foolish."

She thought so too. Why would he blackmail the killer over telling the police? If he had seen all of that happen, why had he never said anything?

"His death was no accident, was it?" she asked Leslie.

"No." He shook his head. "This couldn't have been the first note he sent. How would he remember who to blackmail and for how much?"

"Maybe he kept a ledger?" Bridget piped up. "If I was trying to keep track of how much money I wanted people to pay me, that's what I would do."

Leslie nodded. "There was a journal in his room. It seemed like he was planning out his days but it would make sense if he wrote it in code."

"Maybe it'll point towards who killed them both," Thea muttered, wringing her hands. Her stomach twisted into knots. A killer was on the loose and everyone thought it was safe. They thought that it was all just a mistake. They had no idea.

"The ball is going to happen tonight as planned." He glanced at her. "We can't let on that anything's wrong."

"I understand," Thea said.

Leslie frowned. "I'm going to go talk to Inspector Anderson. Maybe he'll give me an idea of where the investigation is at."

"Of course." She forced a smile on her face, even though she felt like she might be sick.

He nodded and left.

It was probably silly of her to go out to the tower without telling anyone, especially with a murderer running around. She didn't know who to ask to go with her. Bridget was too upset. Leslie was busy with Inspector Anderson. James was still being questioned.

Could James have actually killed someone? It wasn't that preposterous an idea. He had shot the murderer on the train. He seemed like he could easily shoot the younger Mr. Livingston.

But what was James' motive? Was Mr. Livingston blackmailing him like he'd blackmailed Bridget's father?

The ground floor didn't seem to have any loose stones or hidden levers. The fireplace there never worked, not the way the one on the first floor did. Still, Thea ducked inside and tried to find something that suggested there was a false panel.

"What are you looking for?"

She shrieked, stomping her heel into the foot of the man standing behind her. He hissed. She ducked and turned around.

James clutched his foot.

"You scared me!" Thea felt overcome with the sudden urge to smack him.

"I was cleared. I came to tell you."

"That's wonderful news."

"I saw you come out here. What are you doing?"

Thea fidgeted slightly. Should she tell him?

"There's supposed to be a treasure hidden out here."

James perked up. "Treasure? What kind of treasure?"

Thea shook her head. "I couldn't find anything about it."

He eyed her. "Show me where you found the maid."

Thea nodded and led him to the fireplace upstairs. James looked inside, pulled the lever that Thea indicated, and opened the compartment. He stepped inside and Thea winced. It somehow seemed wrong to be in a place that had served as a grave for so long.

It felt colder suddenly. Thea pulled her jacket tight around her body to shield from the chill in the air, but it did little good.

James emerged a minute later.

"There was nothing in there." He shook his head. "If there was something there, it's long gone."

CHAPTER EIGHTEEN

"I can't believe they're still going to have the ball tonight, my lady," Bridget said as she twisted strands of Thea's hair into some sort of intricate design and pinned it in place with diamond hairpins.

Thea's mind was still set on the tower. She and James had searched the rest of it. They found other hidden compartments, but there wasn't anything in those either. Was the treasure even real to begin with? Had Kate been killed over nothing?

"It feels sort of vulgar, doesn't it?" Thea shook her head, ignoring Bridget's glare as she did so.

"Please stay still, my lady."

She pressed her lips together, fighting a laugh.

The gown she wore was a deep blue, the color of the loch reflecting the early morning light off its waters. The silk was covered in a thousand tiny crystals that all seemed to catch the light and shimmer as she moved. The train, thankfully, wasn't long enough to trip on as she danced but it was long enough to make an entrance. Molly had made a good choice in the gown for Thea.

Bridget stepped back, allowing Thea to stand up and admire herself in the mirror. She looked stunning, like someone who actually commanded the attention of others when she came into the room. She looked confident for a change. She looked like someone who deserved to stand by Leslie's side.

"You look lovely, my lady."

She beamed. "Thank you."

Mercury stumbled forward, tripping over his own feet as he made his way over to see what all the fuss was about. He rubbed his cheek along it before he lifted a paw and batted the beads on the bottom of the dress.

"I think Mercury agrees." Bridget stooped down and picked up the kitten, stroking his ears. He meowed unhappily, glaring at her for thwarting his attempts to climb Thea's gown.

Thea smiled and ran a hand over Mercury's head. The kitten purred, pleased with this at least.

BRIDGET'S EFFORTS WERE NOT WASTED ON LESLIE. AS THEA descended the stairs, she could see his eyes grow wide. The main hall doubled as the ballroom during large, formal events. The room had been transformed into something from a fairy story. Candles twinkled from the chandeliers, the walls glowed with the light, and people spun around the dance floor in a sea of swirling colors.

The room was filled by more guests than Thea ever remembered seeing. The last time she had been there, she was too young to join in the ball. She and Charlie had escaped their minder and watched from between the balusters of the balcony overlooking the hall. From above, the whole affair had a sort of magic to it, like a painting come to life.

Leslie held out his hand and Thea took it as she reached

the ground, wishing she wasn't wearing gloves so she could feel his skin against hers again.

"Would you do me the honor of this dance?"

"It would be my pleasure," she said softly, squeezing his hand as they walked to the floor.

The music from the orchestra had echoed loudly in the upstairs gallery but here, the sound flowed softly down, adding a layer of enchantment to an otherwise horrible day. It was a beautiful way to forget that there was a killer among them.

Uncle Malcolm led Aunt Diana around the dance floor. Several couples spun gracefully, the ladies' gowns glittering in the dim light.

Josiah Thayne approached them as they stood on the edge of the dance floor. When Leslie saw him, he smiled at his older brother.

"Leslie, Lady Theodora," Josiah greeted, his accent much thicker than his brother's. He took Thea's hand and kissed her knuckles. Leslie's eyes narrowed. "Do you mind if I have a dance later?"

"Of course." She smiled and he headed off to go dance with Charlie.

Leslie offered her his hand and led her out to the floor, spinning her as they went. The dance that everyone was doing was fast paced, jumping up on their toes and moving so that the other couples were nothing more than blurs as they passed by.

Dancing with Leslie felt a little like flying, or as close as she would ever get.

But then one of the figures seemed to move towards her and bumped into her. She gasped.

"Are you all right?" he asked as they slowed their steps.

She nodded, even though she was finding it a bit hard to catch her breath. But that had very little to do with the dancing and more to do with the company. Any one of them could have killed Kate and then the younger Mr. Livingston to silence him.

"Do you need to sit down?"

She shook her head but he didn't listen and guided her to one of the chairs. She took a deep breath as he sat down beside her.

"Would you like to get some air?"

Across the floor, Wilhelmina spun carefully in Anthony's arms, looking like she belonged there. Her husband glared from the side of the room. Seeing her with Anthony made for a striking comparison to that afternoon. Around Anthony, Wilhelmina acted like she had on the train: alive and vibrant. Mr. Livingston seemed to drain the life from her until there was nothing left but a mask.

"Thea?" Leslie asked again. Thea blinked.

"I'm sorry, I don't—"

"Come on," he said, standing again.

He offered her his hand and she took it, allowing him to escort her into the hallway. Away from the music and crowd, it was easier to breathe.

"I'm sorry," she whispered. "I don't know what came over me."

He ran his hands down her arms, brushing over the smooth leather of her gloves. His fingers caught slightly on the buttons at the wrist. She breathed deeply, inhaling his cologne.

"It's all right to be afraid," he said soft enough that even if they had been around others, they wouldn't have heard. A thrill went through her at the word. His hands met hers and their fingers intertwined. "But nothing is going to happen to you while you're with me."

He squeezed her hands tightly in his.

"I know," she whispered, her voice coming out weaker than she planned. She swallowed.

"Do you want to go back inside?"

"Yes. I think so."

He gave her a look that filled her with warmth. She wrapped her arms around his arm as he led her back inside. She did feel safe with him. She knew he wouldn't let anything happen to her.

CHAPTER NINETEEN

IT TOOK LONGER FOR JOSIAH TO APPROACH HER THAN THEA thought. He managed to wait until his set after Uncle Malcolm finished dancing with her before he made his appearance. It surprised her that he would wait. What few interactions she'd had with him felt like he'd sized her up and found her lacking in some regard.

"Lady Theodora," Josiah greeted again as he bowed to her but the motion felt somewhat mocking. She curtsied slightly and took his offered hand as he led her onto the floor.

"Please, call me Lady Thea."

"Lady Thea," he amended. "I wondered about that. Most people seem to call you 'Lady Thea,' but Mr. Poyntz calls you 'Lady Theodora' mostly."

"Mr. Poyntz does it to annoy me. He knows I prefer Thea."

Josiah chuckled, his laugh very much like his brother's. The family resemblance wasn't very hard to find. He was as tall as Leslie but he was broader and his dark hair was more wavy than curled. Most people probably said that Josiah was the handsome one of the two. He looked like a statue from Ancient Greece.

He stayed silent for a few turns, moving in time to the music.

"Please be careful with my brother," Josiah requested as they swayed on the floor.

"Careful?"

"I've never seen him like this with anyone." He glanced around the room and his voice dropped. "Just... please don't break his heart."

"I won't," she promised.

She had no intention of trying to hurt him.

"Let me go!"

The cry erupted abruptly from the other side of the room. Josiah froze and Thea turned as the music stopped. Mr. Livingston, the alive one, grabbed at his wife. Wilhelmina twisted away from her husband's touch. From her spot, she could see him hiss something that made his wife flinch back.

Livingston made another attempt to snatch her arm but Wilhelmina pulled out of his reach and stormed from the room, apparently unaware and uncaring of the scene she'd caused. Livingston's face darkened as she left, and he followed after her.

When he left the room, it was like everyone was taking a collective sigh. Something about their mysterious argument had been so heavy that it felt like a weight laid across the room.

"What do you think that was about?" James asked as he approached them.

Thea shook her head. "Certainly nothing good."

"Do you mind if I cut in?" her brother asked Josiah.

The Scotsman stared at her, as if trying to find something in her face. Whatever it was, he must have found it because he nodded and stepped back. James took her hand and placed the other on her waist, twirling her softly as they went.

He leaned in so he could be heard over the music. "I've been officially cleared."

"I heard."

He clearly had more practice at reading her expressions than she thought. He studied her face for a long moment and spoke again, "What's wrong?"

"Why would you think anything's wrong?" she asked, forcing a smile on her face. Inside, she still felt sick.

James raised his brow and she sighed.

"My maid found a blackmail note that Francis Livingston wrote to Kate's killer but never sent out."

"A note," he repeated. His face took on a greenish tint.

"It was for someone who was going to be here today. He wanted them to deliver the money tonight to the garden."

His eyes narrowed.

"Do you have this letter?"

Thea shook her head. "Inspector Thayne has it."

"Does he?" He pulled away. "Please excuse me."

"Where are you going?"

"Where do you think, Theodora?"

She linked her arm with his. "Then I'm going with you."

CHAPTER TWENTY

"Inspector," James said as the inspector danced with Emma. "A word if you don't mind."

Emma's eyes narrowed. The gesture was so similar to James' that Thea had to blink. She had accepted him so readily as her brother that she forgot he had a life before he came into hers.

Leslie glanced at Thea, then turned briefly to Emma. "Excuse me, Miss Poyntz."

He bowed his head and the three of them headed out to the balcony.

The air outside was frigid. Thea wished she had grabbed her coat. She rubbed her hands up her arms and wished the gloves were thicker. Even a shawl would have been helpful.

"What was so important that you needed to talk to me now?"

"Livingston's death wasn't a hunting accident." James crossed his arms. "He was blackmailing others, not just the maid's killer, wasn't he?"

Leslie glared at Thea and she ducked her head, even as he drily replied, "I wonder where you could have heard that."

"It's James." She shivered hard enough that her teeth chattered.

Leslie slipped his jacket off, wrapping it around her. It was still warm from him.

James clenched his jaw. "What did you do with this note?"

"I asked his man to deliver it as usual."

"And did his man know who it was going to?"

Leslie shook his head. "No. He told me he couldn't deliver it."

James frowned.

"However, he did tell me that Mr. Livingston had sent out another such note yesterday evening. He didn't get a good look at it but Livingston got rather angry that he'd even seen it. Apparently that note was vaguer than the one found in his room but it still listed where and what time to deliver the money."

"And what time was that?"

"Nine."

James reached into his pocket and flipped the cover on his watch. "It's nearly nine. They should be coming out any minute."

"I'll go look," Leslie said but James snickered as if to let the policeman know exactly what he thought of the idea of him going alone.

"Lead the way, Inspector."

Leslie glanced at Thea. "You should head back inside. We'll be back shortly."

Thea rolled her eyes. They didn't know her very well if they thought she was content to stay inside. "I'm coming with you."

Leslie looked to James, as if he expected her brother to agree with him but James merely shrugged and gave the inspector a smile. Resigned, Leslie sighed and nodded and the three of them headed towards the East Garden. In the moonlit night, there was no one to be seen. But a small bag was already sitting under the angel statue.

"We're too late," Thea whispered, the words like a hit to her stomach.

Leslie knelt down and pulled the bag open. It was filled to the brim with banknotes.

"Perhaps there are fingerprints on the banknotes," James suggested. "The Americans have used that method successfully to identify people. It might work with this as well."

"And I suppose you just happen to know how to do that, Mr. Poyntz?"

"Don't they teach anything at Scotland Yard?" James snipped back.

"Enough." Thea glared at them both. "Let's head back inside. I doubt the person stayed out here."

But even as she said the words, the shine of something in the shadows made her flinch.

"Get down!" she cried and grabbed at their sleeves to yank them down. A bullet whirled past their heads and embedded itself in the statue. They dove behind the angel as a second shot fired.

"You don't happen to have a gun, do you, Mr. Poyntz?"

"No. You, Inspector?"

"Upstairs, for all the good that does us now."

A third shot fired. James didn't seem to care. He stood up and rushed in the direction that it came from. Thea went to stand, to grab him but Leslie held onto her tightly, keeping her behind the statue.

She waited for a fourth shot. The silence was deafening. Her heart pounded against her ribcage. Why had it gone quiet?

"You can come out now," James' voice came. "He's gone."

He stood over a spot where footprints were embedded into the dirt. The hedge in front of it had been smashed down, perhaps as a spot to rest the gun. But there was no one else in sight.

———

"DO YOU STILL THINK THIS WAS JUST AN ACCIDENT, INSPECTOR Anderson?" James growled at Inspector Anderson, his arms crossed over his chest, looking eerily like their mother had when Thea had gone to stay with her cousin in northern Hampshire without telling her where she was going.

"I'm sure you've figured out that I never actually thought that." He glanced over at Constable Mitchell, who was busily trying to dig the bullet out the statue. "We thought that the person who did it might feel more comfortable, you know, thinking that he or she was safe from suspicion, and might make a mistake."

"Bloody comfortable, all right," he muttered. "What the devil made you think this was a good idea?"

"Really, Mr. Poyntz, there's no need for such language," Inspector Anderson chided. He spared a wary glance at Thea.

"I was kind of wondering the same thing myself," Leslie said as he joined them. "I would have liked to have known what you were planning."

The older inspector flushed in the moonlight. "With all due respect—"

"No," Leslie snapped, surprising Thea with his harshness. "If I had known what you were doing, none of us would have been nearly killed tonight."

"I'm sorry that happened, Mr. Thayne but—"

"If you had just been upfront with me—"

"Excuse me," Constable Mitchell approached. "I think you should go inside. Especially Lady Theodora. This is no place for a lady."

Thea wanted to tell the man exactly how she felt about

Inspector Anderson and his ideas but James had already voiced her thoughts on the matter.

"Of course, *Inspector.*" James sneered. "We'll get out of your way. Come along, Theodora. We've been dismissed," her brother snarled, storming towards the house. Leslie and Thea exchanged a glance and followed after him. There was no telling what he'd get up to if left to his own devices.

He stopped on the doorstep, looking very much like he'd like to hit something.

"Bloody Scots," James muttered under his breath before glancing back at Leslie. "No offense, Thayne. You're not a bad sort. It's just those two…"

He made a vague gesture, waving towards the garden as his voice trailed off.

Leslie snickered. "None taken."

"I've never dealt with such incompetence in my life."

"That's an understatement." The inspector glanced at Thea before he reached for the door, resting his hand on the handle. "How did you know to duck?"

Thea blinked. "What?"

"He's right," James said softly. "Just before the first bullet, you told us to 'get down.'"

She shook her head, trying to clear it. "I saw something. It was just a flash."

Leslie and her brother shared a look.

"The barrel?"

"Maybe," the inspector replied. "Was it shiny?"

"Silvery."

They looked at each other again. Leslie frowned. "Livingston's gun was unfinished like that. The younger. Anyone could have taken it to use."

Leslie pulled the door open and let them both go inside.

"Anyone could have used it but would they have been able

to put it back?" James asked, "Or would they still have it? If they do, maybe we can catch them with it."

But even as he said it, they all knew it was a long shot. They were hoping for anything that might help identify the killer.

CHAPTER TWENTY-ONE

THE THREE OF THEM STOOD AWKWARDLY IN THE HALLWAY, avoiding each other's eyes. The tension was palpable, hanging heavily in the air around them. The music from the ball had lost the magical appeal from before and now echoed through the castle's halls, a haunting song that seemed to encapsulate the darkness of the day. Thea swallowed.

James lifted a hand, running his fingers through his hair. "What an utter mess."

"It truly is," Thea whispered, leaning against the table. She didn't think she could stand on her own at the moment. Her legs felt like they might give out. She supposed being shot at for the first time did that to a person.

Leslie shook his head as he paced. His fists clenched and unclenched by his side.

"You're shaking like a leaf," her brother noted. Leslie paused his movements, turning to take in her appearance.

She straightened automatically. She wasn't a damsel in need of rescuing. This wasn't the first time she'd been in danger. There was no reason she was acting this way. She gripped the bottom of Leslie's jacket until her knuckles turned white, until her hands stopped shaking. She shook her head. "I'm fine."

"I should take you to your room."

"*I'll* see her upstairs," Leslie told James as he stepped towards her, leaving no room for argument.

James raised his eyebrow at him, as if to tell him exactly what he thought of that. Leslie ignored him and offered his arm, like he knew she wouldn't be able to keep upright by herself.

Once they started walking, she felt a little better. Her heart was still pounding wildly in her chest and she forced herself to breathe deeply.

"You didn't have to bring me up," she told him. Any other night she might have been glad but tonight, she felt like she was a child being coddled.

When he spoke, his voice was soft enough that she had to lean closer to hear him. "I wanted to."

She inhaled sharply, looking up at him.

"You were brave out there."

Thea shook her head. "I hid behind a statue."

"I said brave, not stupid. Stupid would have been running towards the shooter." The words 'like James did' went unsaid. "But if you hadn't spotted him when you did, tonight might have gone differently."

"The killer still got away."

"And we'll find him tomorrow."

"You're going to let me help?" she asked, a bit surprised. He had fought her tooth and nail any time she got involved, or at least, let his displeasure at the idea be known. Was he really going to step back and let her involve herself in the investigation?

"It doesn't do any good when I ask you to stay away, so yes, you can help." Thea grinned up at him and he fought a smile, clearly trying to act more serious. "At least that way, I'll be able to keep an eye on you.

They paused when they reached her door and she turned the knob. The room was dark, the curtains drawn tight.

"I guess Bridget hasn't been up to light the candles yet," Thea said, hesitating in the doorway. She couldn't bring herself to walk inside. Not yet.

"Do you want me to take a look around?"

She felt foolish as she nodded but Leslie's expression never changed. He walked into the room while she stayed in the hallway, using the wall to support herself. It was incredible how the moment she stood still, she felt shaky again. After another minute, Leslie returned to the hallway.

"It's fine. No one's in there."

She let out a breath of relief.

"Thea," he started but she shook her head.

"I'm fine." He didn't seem to believe her. "I will be fine."

"I can stay, if you want," he offered, looking as nervous as she felt, "at least until Bridget gets here."

She shook her head. It wouldn't be proper or appropriate. He was a guest in her family's home. If he waited in her bedroom, it would probably start a scandal she'd never live down. "Really, I'll be all right. You should go back to the party."

"If you're sure," he said skeptically.

"I am." She licked her lips. "I'm probably just going to get some rest. It's been a long day."

He nodded. She pulled his jacket off of her shoulders and handed it to him.

"Of course. Goodnight, Thea."

"Goodnight, Leslie."

He hesitated, looking very much like he wanted to reach out to her. But he didn't. Instead, he turned away. As she watched him go, she wished more than anything that he'd been able to stay and she could feel the blood rush to her cheeks at that thought.

He glanced back, watching from a few paces away until she shut the door. She locked it and moved to sit down at her desk. The dim light from the fireplace and the candle Leslie had lit cast shadows on the walls but she didn't dare try to light another candle with her nerves.

Why couldn't they have installed electricity in the whole castle yet? she thought. The process seemed to be tedious and they only had it in the rooms on the ground floor. Perhaps by next visit, she could simply flip a switch and not have to pray she didn't trip over Mercury, wherever he was resting.

After spending most of the day in the bathroom, she couldn't bear to leave him in there again, no matter how comfortable she and Bridget tried to make it for him. She only hoped that he didn't get into anything this time. They moved most of it into locked drawers and the wardrobe so that the kitten wouldn't be able to steal anything else.

Thea barely made it across the room to the vanity stool before she collapsed. It felt as if any energy she had vanished the minute she sat down and it became a struggle to keep her eyes open. She peeled her gloves off and dropped them carelessly on the table.

"Meow?" A little head popped up from her vanity, half-hidden beneath gloves and the locked trinket box.

She jumped, clutching her chest. Heart hammering under her hand, Thea took a deep breath, trying to calm herself.

"Hello," she whispered, reaching out to rub the kitten's head. The silky fur did more to help her breathe properly again than she could have imagined. "It's been a long day."

He made a sympathetic sound, as if he could understand what she was saying. *Could he?*

A yawn cut off anything she might have said next. Mercury cocked his head.

"I know I should go to bed but I need to wait for Bridget," she told him. She yawned and he mimicked. His tongue darted out as he blinked several times. "She should be here any minute."

She kept rubbing at the spot on his head between his ears. He seemed to enjoy that. His eyes grew heavy and he rested his chin on his paws.

"I know," she whispered. "We need to stay awake just a little bit longer."

THE SOUND OF SOMETHING JIGGLING IN THE LOCK MADE THEA jump from where she had dozed. She reached blindly around for the closest weapon she could find, one of her parasols, and held it up like it was a cricket bat, ready to strike. She moved behind the wardrobe, waiting for the person to come closer. She wasn't going to make it easy for them to get her.

Where was Bridget? Why hadn't she come yet?

The person came farther into the room, setting something down on the table closest to the bed as Thea crept forward. Something rattled, sounding a bit like porcelain?

Bridget turned and shrieked.

"Good grief!" Thea cried, lowering the parasol. "You scared me half to death."

"I scared you, my lady?" the maid asked incredulously. She lit one of the lamps, then another.

On the table sat a tray with a teapot, cup, and saucer. That had to have been what she heard.

"Why did you bring tea?"

"I ran into Inspector Thayne in the hallway," Bridget admitted. "He told me that you needed this and that you were to drink the whole pot."

"He had you put sugar in it, didn't he?"

The maid looked down, looking a bit guilty. A sip of the tea confirmed it. Thea shook her head, feeling a bit fond of the inspector, even as she grimaced at the taste of the tea.

"I could get you a new pot, my lady," the maid offered.

"No. According to the inspector, drinking sugary tea is good for a shock."

Bridget smiled, as if she didn't quite know what to make of that.

"My lady," Bridget asked, "are you all right?"

Thea almost nodded, almost said that yes, she was fine. Instead, she shook her head.

She had nearly been killed because someone had decided that she, Leslie, and James were the blackmailers. Which didn't even make any sense since neither she nor Leslie had been there when Kate was killed. Perhaps the person assumed that James was the real blackmailer?

As her hands started to shake, she set the cup and saucer back onto the table, collapsing into the chair.

"Someone shot at us in the garden."

Bridget's eyes went wide and she whispered something under her breath.

"None of us were hurt," she told the maid before she could ask, "but I suppose that up until this point, the whole experience was sort of surreal."

"It does all sound like something from a penny dreadful."

Thea laughed, the sound coming out hollow and bitter to her ears.

"It'll all turn out fine though, my lady, you'll see."

She wished she had Bridget's optimism. Perhaps it would have made the whole experience easier. Perhaps not.

"Would you like me to stay the night?" the maid offered as she went about straightening up things that hardly needed to be, just so that she looked like she was busy.

"Would you?" Thea asked. She didn't want to be alone.

Logically, she knew it didn't make sense that the killer would come after her but that didn't help her feel any better.

Bridget nodded. "If it's all right with you, I'll just go get my nightclothes and I'll be back to help you undress."

"Of course." She let out a sigh of relief. "That'll be fine."

The maid gave her a small smile and walked out the door. As she did, Thea slumped in her chair, as much as her corset would allow. As soon as Bridget came back, she would lock the door and sleep with it locked tonight. There was no sense in making it easy for anyone to get in.

DESPITE THE LATENESS OF THE HOUR, MUSIC CARRIED THROUGH the door. The balls Thea had been to usually lasted until well past midnight and this one probably was no exception.

She groaned. It would be into the early hours before the noise stopped.

Bridget sat curled up in the chairs by the fire. Her bare toes stuck out from under the thin blanket. She appeared to be daydreaming, staring off at the door.

Mercury was curled up on the pillow on the other side of the bed. That seemed to be his preferred spot and he had made a little nest of one of the small blankets Bridget brought for him.

Thea pushed the blankets back, sitting up carefully as to not wake him. She was too restless to sleep. The day had too much excitement and her heart still hadn't slowed down. She stood, slid her feet into her slippers, and headed towards the window and pushed the curtain back.

She could see the village from there. Some of the houses still had candles lit. The moon sparkled on the water of the loch. If she didn't know any better, she would say that the night was peaceful.

Turning back towards the maid, Thea said, "You could take the bed. I'm probably not going to get any sleep tonight."

Bridget shook her head. "Thank you, my lady, but I'm fine."

She brought her knees up closer and Thea almost argued but figured that it wouldn't do her any good.

"Do you think that they'll try anything else tonight, my lady? The killer, I mean?"

Thea shook her head. "I don't know. I really hope not."

She leaned her head against the cool windowpane. It helped stave off some of the headache forming behind her temple and the throbbing deep into her skull.

"You should try to get some rest, my lady," Bridget told her. "I'll wake you if anything happens."

Thea nodded and crawled back between the sheets. Mercury shifted over, snuggling against her shoulder. This time, she was asleep before her head touched the pillow.

CHAPTER TWENTY-TWO

"THEA?" SOMEONE WHISPERED OUTSIDE THE DOOR. THE ROOM was still shroud in darkness, save for the dim light of the dying fire.

Instantly, Thea was upright in her bed, wide awake and alert. Across the room, Bridget's shadowed figure reached blindly for a weapon for whatever good it would do. Mercury hissed unhappily at being disturbed.

The door banged in the frame as someone outside jiggled the door handle.

"I know you're in there, Thea," Charlie's voice came. "Let me in."

Thea took a deep breath, trying to calm herself.

"I'm coming," she called, pushing herself out of the bed.

She crossed the room, still able to hear the music's soft melody through the wood, and opened the door. In the hallway, Charlie swayed, stumbling on the hem of her dress. She nearly fell as she walked into the room. Thea blinked in confusion. It was unlike Charlie to be so clumsy or ungraceful.

"Have you been up here all night?" her cousin asked.

"Are you all right?"

Charlie waved off her concern. "You disappeared."

"What?"

"At the ball," the girl stated, like Thea should have been able to follow the conversation. "You disappeared with the handsome Inspector and Mr. Poyntz at the ball. But then they came back and you didn't."

Thea blinked and took a deep breath. She started choking. The smell of alcohol overwhelmed her.

"Charlie," she said slowly, "Have you had much to drink tonight?"

Charlie frowned and shook her head. "I didn't drink anything." She shook her head again. "I wish I had."

"But you smell like—"

In the darkness, Thea could barely make out Charlie's glare. "Sylvia did it. She poured her entire glass of wine on my dress at dinner. It was an accident, she said."

Charlie scoffed but she sounded closer to tears. Angrily, she wiped at her face with her gloved hands.

Thea stared. As her eyes adjusted, she saw the dark stain on the girl's ivory dress. It didn't seem like it would come out easily.

"Some accident," her cousin muttered. "She did it on purpose."

Thea sighed and wrapped her arm around Charlie, leading her to a chair to sit before she fell again.

"Why did she do that?"

"Because she was angry that I talked to Mr. Poyntz at dinner. I asked him about his articles and she just—" Charlie cut off, shaking her head as she hid her face, but Thea could hear the tears in her voice when she started talking again.

"She doesn't sound like a very good friend."

Her cousin scoffed. "She's not my friend. If I never talk to her again, it will be too soon."

"My lady," Bridget said softly, stepping up to them. "We should get you back to your room so you can change."

Charlie nodded and wiped furiously at her eyes.

"I can't go back out there looking like this."

"Here. You can borrow this." Thea reached into the wardrobe and grabbed the first shawl she came across. Charlie wrapped it around herself, holding it so that it mostly covered the dark red stain on the front of her dress.

Thea pulled on her dressing gown, tying the belt tight. With any luck, everybody would still be downstairs.

The three of them moved quickly through the hallway. Charlie pulled the shawl tighter around herself as she glanced back and forth nervously down the hallway. They paused as they reached Charlie's door. Bridget lit the candles on the bedside tables, filling the room with dim light and strangely shaped shadows that danced with the flickering flames.

Bridget moved silently behind Thea's cousin and began undoing the tiny buttons that held the dress closed. Charlie's sniffles filled the room.

"I can't believe she'd do this." Charlie scrubbed at her eyes with a lacy handkerchief. She lifted her arms and allowed Bridget to pull off the ruined gown.

Thea didn't know what she could say to make her feel better. Before Thea was presented, she had never even been to a ball, not even the ones at Astermore.

"You have to go out there and show Sylvia she didn't affect you."

Charlie nodded and left.

Bridget held out the gown. "I'm going to take this to be cleaned."

Thea nodded and headed back to her room.

Her room was quiet when she walked inside, still as dark as they'd left it. She felt a hand wrap around her face and the door shut soundly behind her.

CHAPTER TWENTY-THREE

HEART POUNDING LOUDLY AGAINST HER CHEST, THEA REACHED up to claw at the person grabbing her. Her nails dug into the man's hand as she stomped hard on his foot. The man cursed and Mercury growled. She jerked her elbow back into his stomach. He grunted, letting her go.

"Ow!" She knew that voice.

Thea blinked, turning her head to look back.

"Why do you always go for the feet?" James complained, though she felt it was hardly fair of him to be upset with her.

"What the bloody hell are you doing lurking in my room grabbing me?"

"Language," James chided, a smirk on his face. "Nice outfit."

Even though she already knew what she was wearing, she had to glance down to check again.

"James," Thea warned, crossing her arms. Mercury stumbled closer to Thea, hiding behind her legs. It seemed James' surprise welcome scared the poor kitten just as much as it had scared her.

He sighed, his expression growing serious.

"I came to check up on you after the excitement of tonight. Imagine my surprise to find you gone."

She shook her head. "I was just taking Charlie back to her room."

"Ah," he muttered, making a face as if something smelt particularly awful. "Miss Erskine is quite persistent. And actually, rather ruthless."

Thea rolled her eyes.

"Why did you grab me when I came in?"

James shook his head, not in any mood for joking. "I didn't realize it was you until you tried to crush my foot again."

"Perhaps if you'd stop pulling me into rooms."

"Thea, please."

James ran his fingers through his hair. It was the same nervous tick her mother had when she was upset about something. It was strange to see him do it and understand the reason why.

He took a deep breath before he moved further into the room, taking a seat by the fireplace. Thea pulled one of the small blankets off of the bed and wrapped it around herself. Mercury padded over, hopping up, and settled his head on her lap, looking up expectantly. She ran a hand through his silky fur. There was something rather calming about petting a cat. She had never realized.

"I thought something had happened to you."

"I'm sorry to have frightened you," she apologized. "I really am fine."

"But you don't have to be." His voice was soft as he stared at her. "Two people are dead and we were nearly shot tonight. It's a lot for anyone to process."

It was then she noticed that he seemed more upset by the events of the day than she would have expected. It was strange to think that only that morning, she questioned his motives for caring about her.

It felt stranger still to actually care about what happened to James. She hadn't worried about him the way he had worried about her. But now, knowing what she did, she wanted him to be safe too.

"Why did you run after the shooter?" she asked, fighting the urge to cross her arms. Mercury made a little noise in annoyance, staring up at her, and she began stroking him again. He settled back down and purred.

James stared at a spot to the side of her face. His eyes avoided hers. It was the spot that he looked at when he lied, she had learned. It was close enough to a person's eyes that most people probably wouldn't notice that he wouldn't meet their gaze.

"I don't know."

She stared at him.

"You're not a policeman. You're not a soldier." Thea said using the little bit of information Constable Mitchell had given her about James. She was glad that she had made the effort to look into his past. It was worth it to see the surprise flash in his eyes.

"I—"

"It's not your job to run into danger."

"It's not yours either. But yet you do."

Thea looked away. She couldn't argue with that. She wasn't sure why she did. People she cared about had been hurt and she needed answers as to why.

"Do you know anything more about all of this?" she asked him, changing the subject.

"What do you mean?"

"Do you know who's behind the deaths? The shooting?" He hesitated. "You must have a theory."

James sighed, leaning back in his chair. "None that I can prove. It doesn't do anyone any good if we go around speculating and accusing innocent people."

She crossed her arms, fixing him with a glare. Mercury caught on to her actions, standing and baring his fangs in James' direction. She hoped it was sufficiently intimidating. It seemed to work, because he wilted. His face lost what little color it had. His hands clenched into fists in his lap.

"I received one of those letters last night around midnight." He glanced at the clock. "Yesterday morning, I guess."

Thea blinked. "What did it say?"

James shook his head. "Nothing good."

"Anything incriminating?" He shot her a glare. She shrugged. "The one that Mr. Livingston sent was about a murder."

"Just things I'd rather not be made public. Not even to you."

A chill ran down her spine. A blackmail letter was motive. And it was awfully convenient that the blackmailer died before anyone had to pay. But what could James possibly have done to receive one of those awful notes?

Mercury let out a yawn, his mouth going wide. Before she could help it, she yawned, raising her hand to cover her mouth. Her eyes watered.

"I'm keeping you up." He stood, fighting back a yawn as he did. "I apologize."

"It's fine. I probably won't be able to sleep anyway."

He frowned.

A noise in the hallway made them both jump and glance warily at the door. The noises turned into footsteps and voices from people going to their rooms for the night and Thea let out a breath of relief.

"You probably shouldn't be in here," Thea said softly, aware that someone might pass and hear them talking. She didn't want to be the center of gossip by having a man in her room, a man who most people didn't know was related to her. "People will talk."

But from the expression on his face, James clearly cared very little about that.

"I'm not leaving you alone. Who knows what you might get into? Two incidents in one day—"

"If you're calling us nearly being killed 'an incident'—" Thea started to say but James cut her off again.

"That is exactly my point."

The door banged open but from the way Bridget's face paled, she doubted the maid did that on purpose. Instead, the maid's eyes were wide as she stood in the doorway.

Immediately, James was on his feet. He glanced over to Thea as Bridget scrambled to close the door behind her.

"My lady, there's a man in here," the maid sibilated as if James couldn't hear her. He rolled his eyes.

"I was just leaving."

Bridget watched his movements warily as he left the room. The door closed silently behind him.

"My lady…"

"Please." Thea held up a hand, pausing whatever words the maid might have said.

Wisely, Bridget stayed quiet, instead choosing to go about tidying up the room.

It was only now that James had left that Thea realized that he had never responded why he had chased after the shooter. He always managed to leave without answering her questions.

THE NIGHT WAS TOO STILL NOW. TOO QUIET. IT MADE IT HARD to sleep.

Thea was used to Ravenholm Castle being a safe haven. As

a child, nothing bad ever happened there. But now, she knew that wasn't true.

She shifted in the bed, trying to get comfortable. She didn't know how she would be able to sleep imagining that a mad man could come crashing through her door at any minute welding a weapon.

She blinked. Really, the killer didn't seem too concerned with how he murdered someone. Hitting Kate's head into the wall. Shooting Mr. Livingston. Shooting at James, Leslie, and her in the garden.

One was up close.

With the second two, the person shooting was able to be farther away.

He would have to be strong and a decent shot.

She ran over the guest list again in her mind. She had memorized it, even though Leslie had confiscated her journal with her notes.

Despite his actions towards Thea herself, she doubted Francis Livingston had killed Kate. But he knew who had and that person more than likely killed him. One of the guests knew who he was, had figured out their blackmailer's identity, and killed him.

Thea closed her eyes for a minute. If she was blackmailing a person who had already killed somebody, she would want to have some sort of insurance in case anything happened. She would want someone she trusted absolutely to have knowledge of what happened, either so they could go to the police and ruin the killer's life or to continue the blackmailing legacy.

She swallowed as she opened her eyes.

Leslie said that Livingston's valet had not known who the person being blackmailed was but perhaps he knew something else. She glanced at the clock on the mantle and saw it was too early to seek him out. She would talk to him herself later in the morning.

Unless the two murders were actually separate incidents. Maybe Francis had killed Kate after all. But then who did he send the note to?

She rubbed her head, trying to will the throbbing pain away. Mercury seemed to think that was his cue to walk onto her face. Thea groaned and picked him up, moving him away from her head. He meowed angrily and settled down so that his tail smacked her ear.

Francis Livingston couldn't have been the one to kill Kate.

That left the rest of the list. Leslie, Josiah, Lord Thayne, and Inspector Anderson hadn't been at the first party. They would have no reason to cover up a murder that they had no part in. And as much as Thea hated to admit it, Inspector Anderson's plan to try to catch the killer hadn't been a bad one, even if it had nearly gotten them killed.

That left only Mr. Erskine, James, his uncle, and Ernest Livingston.

She ruled out James.

She hadn't spent enough time with the other three gentlemen to know. If she were to bet, she would place her money on Wilhelmina's husband being the killer.

Even if that meant he had murdered his own brother.

She sat up in the bed, rubbing at her face. Did Wilhelmina know anything?

Thea stood, careful not to disturb Mercury again, and stretched as she walked towards the fireplace. From the light of the dying embers, she could see that the clock on the mantle read just after four in the morning. She would need to get up in a few hours. She needed to sleep but she couldn't get her mind to stop running over everything that had happened in the last few days.

"My lady?" Bridget's voice came from the chair. "Do you need something?"

"When I asked you to look in Mr. Livingston's room—the older Mr. Livingston—did you find anything?"

She supposed it would be too much to ask for him to have a signed confession laying out on his desk when Bridget searched it.

"No, my lady." She paused. "Well, actually, there was something odd."

"What was it?"

Bridget hesitated. "It was just that his fireplace had ash that, er, looked like paper had been burned in it recently."

"Paper?" Thea repeated dubiously. It was hardly the most suspicious of things.

She could hear Bridget shifting on her makeshift bed. "That was why I didn't mention it earlier, my lady. It didn't seem like anything special. But perhaps it was a letter."

"Like a blackmail letter that he wouldn't want anyone to see," Thea muttered. "I'll talk to Inspector Thayne about it in the morning."

There was nothing either of them could do about it in the middle of the night, even if he was the killer. By now, everyone would have gone to bed and it would be extremely improper to go into the bachelor's wing to wake up Leslie or James to tell her theory. Not that propriety had deterred either man from coming to her bedroom.

She was still tempted to but her need for sleep outweighed getting back up to track them down. She wasn't sure which rooms they were in. The last thing she wanted to do was wander around the castle at night with a killer on the loose.

Mercury blinked up at her.

"Meow?"

She scratched behind his ears and he dropped his head on her chest. Telling Leslie could wait until morning.

CHAPTER TWENTY-FOUR

Despite her late-night adventure, Thea woke up feeling refreshed. She wished Bridget had felt the same. Dark smudges and bloodshot eyes made her look like some sort of creature from the shadows.

Bridget helped her dress in relative silence. It seemed that the maid's sleeplessness caused her not to be her usual talkative self. Thea felt responsible for that, though she supposed it really was Charlie's fault. If Charlie had gone straight to her room rather than to vent, Bridget and Thea would have slept through the night. James also wouldn't have been waiting to wind her up.

Thea looked up, meeting the eyes of the maid as she stood behind her in the mirror, running the brush through Thea's hair.

"Does Wilhelmina, um, Mrs. Livingston," Thea corrected herself, "have an adjoining room to Mr. Livingston?"

"Yes, my lady."

So it was entirely possible that Wilhelmina might have seen the letter before Mr. Livingston burned it. Perhaps its contents explained why she had been so terrified at the luncheon yesterday.

"I'm going to breakfast. She should be in there."

Wilhelmina ate breakfast with them yesterday morning, despite the fact that married women usually took breakfast in their rooms. Perhaps, being the social creature that she was, she liked to be around people. Or, perhaps, it was like Wilhelmina said on the train. Mr. Livingston tried to control her and wanted to keep an eye on her. Always.

She shuddered at the thought.

Bridget nodded and pushed a pin into Thea's hair. It caught and stabbed her scalp slightly. Thea winced and the girl jerked back.

"I'm so sorry, my lady," the girl apologized. "I don't know what came over me."

Her hands trembled, fingers shaking like tiny earthquakes. Her eyes were glassy, not quite focusing on Thea or anything else.

"You should get some rest after I leave."

Bridget stared blankly at her.

"My lady?"

"I kept you up most of the night." Mercury was hiding under the bed. She had seen him dart under there after she got dressed. It seemed that last night upset him as much as everyone else. Not that Thea blamed him, of course, but she wasn't sure if she was supposed to try to lure him out or leave him be. She opted for the latter and hoped that he would eventually come out.

"There's still work that needs to be done." Of course, there was. Everyone needed to be working and helping where they could. But Bridget would be of no help to anyone, least of all herself, if she was too exhausted to function.

"You can sleep in here if you'd like. I need you awake and alert to help me dress for dinner." After all, it was the last night of the hunt. She needed to look her best. "If you want, I can even tell Mrs. Campbell that I ordered it."

The girl flushed. "No, that's all right, my lady."

Thea stared at her until the maid bowed her head. She would try to catch Mrs. Campbell on the way to breakfast and tell her to let Bridget rest. It was the least she could do.

LESLIE WAS ALREADY AT THE TABLE WHEN SHE GOT DOWNSTAIRS. He smiled at her briefly as he saw her and stood to pull out the chair as she joined him.

"Did you get some sleep last night?" he asked, his voice low so that they wouldn't be overheard.

"Barely. Did you?"

"Not much. I can't stop thinking about last night."

She hoped that Inspector Anderson would have been more competent when it came to investigating. But in the last two days, it all seemed like it was some sort of joke to him. A theater production that he had lost control over.

Across the table, Mr. Livingston set his plate down. Thea doubted she would have been able to carry on if her brother had died in front of her like that. But the man across from her didn't even seem phased.

Perhaps he didn't care. She had heard of people like that, ones that didn't really connect to the people around them, that just used them for as long as they were useful. Perhaps that was why Mr. Livingston seemed so unaffected by everything that had happened.

That thought made her tremble. How dangerous was someone with no regard for anyone around them?

What was truly odd was that he was there without his wife. Throughout the whole trip, Wilhelmina had barely left his side. Where was she now?

"Can we talk after breakfast?" she asked Leslie, leaning closer. No one would think twice about them being close. Everyone assumed they were involved anyway. "Somewhere private?"

"Outside?"

Thea shook her head. After last night, she wasn't entirely comfortable going where someone might hide behind a hedge and take shots at them.

"How about the library?"

Leslie hesitated but nodded. She wondered if he could see the worry on her face.

His hand moved from the table and he tugged her hand towards him. His fingers intertwined with hers and he squeezed. Her heart fluttered, and she held on tighter. "Whatever it is, it'll be fine."

Thea shook her head. "I'm not so sure."

He rubbed his thumb over the back of her hand. "It will be. You'll see."

She tried to believe him.

After they finished breakfast, the men planned to go on a ride. The girls decided to join them. Thea motioned to James as everyone left the dining room. Her brother's eyes flickered to Leslie but he followed after them as they headed towards the library.

Once they were inside, Thea bolted the doors behind.

"What's going on?" her brother asked, glancing between her and Leslie.

Thea ignored him and turned to the inspector. "Did you read everything in my journal?"

Leslie shook his head. "I started but I didn't finish. You took surprisingly thorough notes." He flushed when she and

James stared at him. "I didn't mean that how it sounded. I'm used to reading police notes from some of the greenest constables who are too busy not being sick by the bodies to pay any actual attention."

"And she didn't even steal mine this time," James drawled. Thea rolled her eyes.

"Anyway," Thea interrupted before the two of them could start again, "as I was saying, in my journal, there were some papers Bridget and I found hidden in her room about treasure."

"The treasure you were looking for in the tower?" her brother asked.

"You went out to the tower?" Leslie asked. "By yourself?"

"I followed her. There was nothing in there," James told him.

Leslie stared between them.

"I'm sure Kate took the notes from someone else." Thea glanced. "Anthony told me the treasure is something of a family legend."

"You think Kate went looking for treasure and was killed by the person she took the notes from," the inspector said as he glanced back at the door. He ran a hand over his face. "That makes a surprising amount of sense."

James crossed his arms. "What exactly do these notes say?"

"I'll go get them," Leslie offered, heading towards the door.

Thea sat down on the couch at the end closer to the fireplace. Her hands were freezing. She wasn't sure if it was from the cold or from everything else.

James sat down across from her, rubbing his hands together. His posture seemed to mimic hers. "Did you sleep at all last night?"

"Did you?" she shot back, right before she yawned. He raised his eyebrows at her as if she had given him exactly the answer that he expected.

"You should probably get some rest."

Thea crossed her arms, sulking a little. "I'll rest when there's not a madman running around the house trying to kill everyone."

"Oh come now, let's be fair," he chastised teasingly. "It could be a madwoman."

"Yes but the only woman who had a gun when Mr. Livingston was shot was Lady Thayne. Surely you don't think that she is the one who tried to kill us."

That shut James up quickly.

"Perhaps there are a few holes in that theory." He leaned back, looking far too comfortable and relaxed for anyone who had been accused of murder only the day before. "Maybe it is Mr. Livingston. But then that means he murdered his own brother. I sure hope you aren't taking notes and planning on doing that with me."

"James," she growled, not finding his gallows humor nearly as comical as he did.

"Yes, little sister?"

A small, high squeak came from behind one of the shelves. Thea's eyes went wide. The two of them jumped from the couch and turned in that direction.

"I think we have a mouse," her brother commented wryly as Thea moved to the panel and pressed the button to release the false panel.

Charlie stumbled out from behind the bookcase, holding on tightly to the end of it.

"Sorry," she blushed, her eyes on the rug. "I wasn't listening."

But she definitely had been. It was obvious from the way she refused to meet either of their eyes.

"I find that very hard to believe." James offered her a hand and guided her to the end of the couch.

"Are you really… was that just a joke?" Charlie stuttered out.

"What?" Thea asked.

"That you're… that he's… are you two really…?"

James stared at her looking more than a bit amused. "Are you trying to ask if our dear Lady Theodora is really my sister?"

Charlie nodded, still not looking at either of them for longer than a second.

"She is," James confirmed.

"At least according to him."

Her cousin's brow furrowed as her nose crinkled. "But how?"

"We share a mother."

"But not a father?" James and Thea both shook their heads. "So we're not related then."

"No," James confirmed.

"Huh." Which seemed to be all that her cousin would say on that at the moment.

Her brother knelt before Charlie, taking her hands in his. He smiled, his lips quirking a little higher on one side than the other. She forgot that James could be charming when he wanted. "How about we just keep this between us?"

"All right." The word was soft, barely above a whisper.

Which was when Leslie walked back into the room, Thea's journal in his hands. He eyed Charlie sitting on the couch, James crouched before her like he was comforting a child, and Thea hovering over both of them. It had to make for quite the picture.

"What happened?" Leslie asked.

Charlie stared at him.

CHAPTER TWENTY-FIVE

Thea had a headache. She wasn't sure how much of it was actually from the lack of sleep. It seemed more likely that it was from them trying to figure out how to get concrete proof that it was the elder Mr. Livingston who killed his brother and Kate. Thea told them that the suspect list was down to only a few people if Mr. Livingston hadn't done it. There was only Mr. Erskine and James' uncle.

"My uncle is not a rampaging maniac!"

"I never said he was," Thea defended.

James leaned forward. "Mr. Erskine fell during the hunt and broke his leg. I remember because I had to help carry him back to the house. At the ball, he complained the entire night that it was pointless for him to sit there and watch."

Thea nodded. "So he couldn't have killed Kate."

"And I'm glad you eliminated me and realized that I wouldn't shoot at myself."

"We do have to consider every angle," Leslie said in mock seriousness, rubbing his chin.

Charlie nodded, adopting a look of perfect sincerity. "I suppose with the right tools, you probably could have made it so the gun could have fired without anyone being there to pull the trigger. After all, if men can fly?"

James glared at them. "I hate you all."

Charlie snickered.

"I didn't kill anyone!" James declared. "I especially didn't try to shoot myself, despite the *absolute faith* you have in me. But if you," he jabbed a finger in Thea's direction, "came up with such an idiotic idea, then I shudder to think what Tweedledum and Tweedledee have come up with."

He was talking about Inspector Anderson and Constable Mitchell. Thinking about it now, it was strange how incompetent the men acted. That hadn't been her first impression of either of them. They had seemed professional and they had asked all the right questions. Perhaps this really was an act to make the killer comfortable so that they would make a mistake.

Thea fought the urge to reach out and take Leslie's hand where it rested between them on the couch. Holding his hand at breakfast, after she had gotten past the initial shock of it, had been calming, soothing. With everything that had happened in the last week, her nerves were rather done for.

Instead, she reached for her journal and opened the notes again.

"Have any of you seen Wilhelmina?" she asked suddenly, interrupting whatever they were discussing.

"What?" Three pairs of eyes stared at her.

"I haven't seen her since last night, and I wanted to ask her about her husband." Thea clenched her fingers. She felt foolish for not thinking of it before.

"You think he knows about the treasure!" Charlie exclaimed, jumping up.

Leslie looked to her cousin. "Why would he know?"

"Ernest and Francis are our cousins from our father's side," Charlie explained. "Ernest spent a lot of time in the tower when I was younger. I remember he and Francis had a big fight about money, not too long before he married Jennie."

They were part of the family. Lady Livingston would have known the family legends since she was Uncle Malcolm's sister.

"They were always trouble. If they weren't Aunt Emily's sons, Mother would have never invited them."

James leaned forward.

"It could be nothing," Charlie said. "Coincidence?"

"In a murder?" Leslie shook his head. "It's not likely."

It was interesting that the tower's plans didn't show any of the compartments that she and James had found. But someone had added about those hidden spaces in the handwritten notes.

Leslie picked up the papers. "I'm going to keep these as evidence."

"I'm going to look for Wilhelmina."

"I'll go with you." Leslie offered her his hand to help her up. She took it and they headed out the door.

AFTER GETTING THE NAME OF THE ROOM FROM MR. SEMPLE, Thea and Leslie searched for and finally found Wilhelmina's room. If it hadn't been for the nameplates on the door, they might not have found it at all. She thought that the idea of naming the rooms was absolutely clever.

The Queen Anne room sat next to the Prince George room. The pair of rooms had doors recessed from the halls, unlike the majority of the rooms in that wing. She was sure there was some historical reasoning as to why but she had never thought to ask before.

Thea wondered which earl and his wife had decided to name all the guest rooms after Scottish Monarchs. If she were to bet, she would say it had been Great Aunt Mary's decision. She had a sense of humor about these sorts of things. Even

Thea's room bore the name Queen Mary, with the room next to it being William of Orange. Her aunt used to tease her that one day, when Thea was married, the William of Orange room would be her husband's. Thea had scowled at such a suggestion and firmly bolted the adjoining door in the shared bathroom years ago.

"Mrs. Livingston?" Thea called as she knocked on the door, aware that others might hear her and question if she used the other woman's first name. She glanced down the hallway but no one was around except for Leslie. When there was no answer, she tried again. "Wilhelmina, are you there?"

It seemed so unlike the other woman not to open her door.

She pressed her ear against it but it was silent inside. Thea moved back and turned the handle. It wasn't too much of a surprise when it didn't open.

"Let me," Leslie muttered, and she stepped back before he knocked solidly against the door. "Mrs. Livingston?"

She held her breath. Nothing.

Thea sighed in defeat. She should have had Bridget show her how she opened a locked door. It would have come in useful. Briefly, she wondered if James would know how.

In the pit of her stomach, she knew something wasn't right but she had no idea what it could be. She needed to know if Wilhelmina was all right.

She pivoted, even as Leslie still faced the door, and came face to face with the last person she'd like to see.

"Mr. Livingston. I thought you went out riding with the men," Thea greeted, feeling her stomach twist to knots as she did so. "We were looking for Mrs. Livingston. Is she around?"

"I'm afraid she's not feeling well," Mr. Livingston said. "I think it might be best if we head home early." He plastered a look on his face, something that Thea thought was supposed to be upset but looked more like he'd eaten something particularly sour.

"Oh! But if she's not well, of course you should stay. I'll call for the doctor."

"That's really not necessary."

"Oh no, I insist. She really shouldn't be traveling if she's not well. I'll call for the doctor." She gave him the sweetest smile she could muster up before she fled.

Thea didn't venture far to find someone to get the village doctor, Dr. Watterson. Thea pushed open one of the guest's rooms doors and found a maid working inside. "Mrs. Livingston has taken ill. Please call for Dr. Watterson and inform Lady Ravenholm what has happened."

"Yes, my lady."

The maid bobbed and scurried from the room. Thea followed her out, moving down the hallway to meet Leslie and Mr. Livingston. In her absence, things between the two men seemed to have grown tense.

She closed her eyes, took a deep breath and summoned her courage before rejoining them.

"I said no, Thayne!" Livingston snapped. He didn't see her since she was approaching from behind.

Leslie's face was hard, the anger evident in his eyes. "And I'm not giving you the option."

"What's going on?" Thea asked, not entirely sure that she wanted to know the answer.

"Mr. Livingston is coming downstairs with me."

She glanced between the two men in confusion. Mr. Livingston clearly wasn't happy but he allowed Leslie to lead him downstairs.

CHAPTER TWENTY-SIX

ONCE THEY WERE OUT OF SIGHT, THEA DUCKED INTO THE alcove and tried the door to Wilhelmina's room again. Unsurprisingly, it was still locked. How could she help if she couldn't even get through a door?

Bridget carried a basket of linens down the hallway, her head down as she passed. Thea reached out and snagged her arm. She didn't want to risk alerting anyone to what she was doing. What if Mr. Livingston wasn't far enough away and heard her?

"My lady?" Bridget asked as she saw who had grabbed her. "What's going on?"

"Can you get this door open?"

Bridget's brow furrowed but she pulled out one of her hair pins and fiddled with it in the knob. After a minute, the door to the darkened room popped open.

"Can you teach me how to do that?" Thea whispered.

"Of course, my lady."

"Later. Not now. Watch the door." Bridget nodded, standing in the hallway, ready to block anyone if they came in.

Thea wished she had grabbed a weapon or something as she walked in. All she had was her journal, for all the good that would do.

The room was dark, the curtains drawn tight and the lamps and fire both out. Thea moved into the room, holding still for a moment to see if she could hear anything. Nothing. She took another step, taking care not to trip in the unfamiliar layout.

She made her way to the window and pulled one of the heavy drapes back. The light flooded the room. Thea flinched and hid her eyes from the sudden brightness.

It was no wonder Wilhelmina hadn't answered the door.

On the floor beside the bed, where no one would have seen her from the doorway, blood poured from her head. Red hand marks colored her wrists. Blood and skin seemed jammed beneath her nails.

Thea dropped to her knees beside her. Her journal fell out of her hands as she tried to find a pulse. Wilhelmina's heartbeat throbbed erratically beneath her fingers.

"Wilhelmina," she whispered, shaking the other woman's shoulder. Thea hoped that she would be all right. "Wake up."

The other woman mumbled something before her eyes blinked open. They were unfocused and Thea didn't like the way that her gaze kept going in and out.

"Careful," Thea said softly as Wilhelmina tried to sit up. With a gentle hand at her shoulder, she pushed Wilhelmina back down. "You hit your head."

"I didn't," she growled. "That monster!"

She continued to mutter several curse words that Thea knew a lady should never say.

"Who?" She was sure it was Mr. Livingston who did this but what if she was wrong?

"E-Ernest," Wilhelmina stammered, lifting her hand to probe at her head and groaning. "He hit me. All over some letter."

He had probably killed Kate. He probably killed his brother to keep him quiet. If she and Leslie hadn't arrived when they did, Wilhelmina would have been his next victim.

Thea took a pillow off of the bed and tucked it under Wilhelmina's head before she knelt back down beside her.

"Do you know if he killed Kate?"

Wilhelmina nodded.

"He killed Francis too. There's no proof," Wilhelmina whimpered. "And I'm his wife. Anything I saw doesn't count…"

Her voice took on a franticness. She took several deep breaths, trying to calm herself. Finally, she looked at Thea. Her eyes glistened with unshed tears.

"I didn't just let him hurt me." Her voice was soft, almost too soft to hear. Thea leaned closer. "He had a knife when he came at me. But I stabbed him with it." She motioned to a spot near her stomach. "Just below his ribs."

At that moment, Doctor Watterson knocked on the door. Thea pushed herself to her feet. Bridget half-blocked the door, glancing between Thea and the doctor.

"May I come in, Lady Theodora?" the doctor asked.

"Yes, please," she motioned and Bridget stepped aside, letting him into the room. "I'm glad you were able to get here so quickly."

Doctor Watterson set his bag beside Wilhelmina as he looked at her head. Thea knelt and squeezed Wilhelmina's hand. "You're going to be all right. He can't hurt you now."

The other woman's eyes were wide again in fear. "But he hasn't confessed."

"He will."

Wilhelmina's expression was doubtful but she didn't hold on as Thea let go of her hand, picked up her journal, and left the room.

"Stay with them," she ordered her maid.

"Yes, my lady." Bridget stepped inside the door and closed it as Thea walked away.

CHAPTER TWENTY-SEVEN

"Leslie?" Thea called out as she saw the inspector leaning against a doorframe. He was barely able to stand. He glanced up, blood dripping down his cheek. She rushed to him and pulled out her handkerchief, pressing it against the long cut that now spanned his forehead. He hissed and she pressed harder. "What happened? Where's Mr. Livingston?"

"He's gone. He threw the vase at my head." He motioned to the pile of shattered glass on the floor. Thea frowned.

"I'll get James and Inspector Anderson. You should sit down."

Leslie shook his head. He didn't look nearly as disoriented as Wilhelmina. Thea wondered how long Wilhelmina had been unconscious. Since breakfast? Since she left the ball last night?

"You shouldn't go alone. Not with him—"

He cut off suddenly. His hand dropped to his side. Panic shot over his face as the color drained from it. For a second, she thought he might pass out.

"What's wrong?"

"He has my gun."

"What?" she asked.

"When Livingston knocked me out, he took my gun."

Her stomach dropped. Thea glanced down the hallway but Livingston wasn't in sight. He'd hardly stick around after taking a policeman's weapon.

"We shouldn't stay here," Leslie muttered, taking the bloodied rag from her hand to press against his head. The blood from the wound didn't seem like it was slowing down.

"You need the doctor."

He shook his head slowly. "Head wounds bleed a lot. It's not nearly as bad as it looks."

Somehow, Thea doubted that. Still, after last night, it'd be better if they went somewhere that wasn't so exposed. She pushed open the door to the drawing room and was relieved to find that Aunt Diana, Great Aunt Mary, Mrs. Erskine, Mrs. Poyntz, and Lady Thayne were inside. Leslie followed behind her, leaning on her more than he probably cared to. Upon seeing them, Leslie's mother was on her feet, crossing the room to help them, ignoring the other women's gasps.

"What on earth happened?" the baroness exclaimed. She wrapped an arm around her son, taking some of his weight from Thea's shoulder.

"Mr. Livingston tried to kill his wife," Thea said as the three of them hobbled to the nearest couch. Leslie all but collapsed.

"And clubbed me over my head and took my gun," the inspector added.

The baroness crossed her arms and glared at her son like she was about to scold him. "And you involved Lady Theodora in this business?"

"She involved herself." He tilted his head back at an angle that looked uncomfortable but did seem to help staunch the flow of blood from the wound.

"I'm going to find Inspector Anderson and James," Thea told him again, despite his previous protest.

"I'll come with you."

"No," Lady Thayne snapped. She glared at him. "You'll stay here."

"I'm perfectly capable of finding them," Thea told him.

"Please be careful."

"I will," she promised before she fled the room.

She didn't actually have to go far. James and Charlie were leaving the library.

"Leslie and I ran into Livingston upstairs but he knocked Leslie out and took his gun." James froze. Charlie went pale. "Have you seen Inspector Anderson?"

"He was interviewing some of the staff."

Thea closed her eyes, taking a deep breath.

"Did you find Mrs. Livingston?" Charlie asked. Thea nodded. "Was she all right?"

Thea shook her head. "Doctor Watterson is with her."

James ran his fingers through his hair. "We need to find Livingston. The idea of him running around armed is not exactly comforting."

Thea glared at him.

"I'll go find the inspector," Thea told them. "Another set of eyes ought to be helpful."

James grimaced but nodded.

FINDING INSPECTOR ANDERSON WAS EASIER THAN THEA WOULD have expected. He was down the hallway, near the servant's door, interviewing one of the maids—a blushing, stuttering girl who had only been at Ravenholm for a year or two. She doubted that the girl knew anything about Kate or Livingston.

"You're sure you don't know anything?" the policeman

asked and Thea fought the urge to scream at him. He couldn't honestly be so oblivious, could he?

"I haven't seen her since the ball last night, sir. I swear."

"Saw who?" Thea asked. She tried to pretend that she wasn't annoyed with him but it was clear from the way the maid's eyes bulged that she failed.

"Mrs. Livingston, my lady," the maid said.

"She's upstairs with Doctor Watterson," Thea said.

Anderson frowned as he turned to her. "What's wrong with her?"

"Her husband hit her over the head. She found a letter from a blackmailer who claimed he saw Livingston kill Kate."

"And Livingston? Was he with her?"

Thea shook her head. "He attacked Inspector Thayne, took his gun, and disappeared."

Inspector Anderson muttered something low under his breath that sounded vaguely like cursing.

"How is Inspector Thayne? Where is he?"

"I found him and took him to the drawing room."

Inspector Anderson pressed his lips together, and she could see the displeasure on his face. She wasn't sure if it was because of Leslie or if it was with the situation in general.

"Right. Then I suggest that's where you go as well."

With that, he stormed away, his footsteps echoing down the hallway. The maid disappeared behind the door.

"What on earth was that about?" James asked as he approached. He carried his shotgun in both hands. If they caught up to Livingston, it would be useful to be armed.

"I just told Inspector Anderson that Mr. Livingston took Leslie's gun."

Knowing Thea wouldn't stay put, James gave her a sardonic grin. "Let's go find ourselves a killer."

CHAPTER TWENTY-EIGHT

Neil, the footman, stood by the front door and looked up as he heard them approaching.

"We're looking for Mr. Livingston," Thea said. It wasn't like the whole house wouldn't know what had happened by dinner time. Gossip spread faster than fires.

"Mr. Livingston just left, my lady." The footman frowned.

"He left?" James repeated as if he couldn't believe what he had heard.

"Yes, sir. He had his car brought around and he drove off." The footman glanced between them. "Is everything all right?"

Thea tried for what she hoped was a reassuring smile. "Everything's fine. Please have Donald bring the car around."

Neil nodded and took off as quickly as he could without running.

"You don't happen to know how to drive, do you?"

James rubbed the back of his neck, looking a little sheepish. "I've tried. I'm afraid I'm not very good. You?"

"Mother wouldn't let me learn." James grimaced.

"I'm not sure I can blame her. You put yourself into enough danger without adding an automobile to the mix."

Thea laughed. "You say that as you come with me to chase a killer."

He shrugged. "Fair point."

James pulled the door open and let her pass. The sun was warm outside.

"After this, I might learn," he said conversationally. "It would be useful to know."

Thea laughed a little at that as Donald, the chauffeur, pulled around the automobile. She only hoped it would be fast enough to catch up with Mr. Livingston.

"My lady, sir," the chauffeur greeted. "Where can I take you?"

"We're following Mr. Livingston's car. Neil said he just left."

Donald nodded. "Only a moment ago."

"What are we going to do when we catch him?" Thea asked James as they sat down. The car bounced along the road as Donald pushed the automobile faster and faster.

Her brother didn't answer.

A black convertible came into sight. Livingston's car, she presumed from the way James straightened. He rolled down the window and leaned out, aiming the shotgun as they drove. Donald glanced back for a second, a nervous look on his face but James hardly paid the man any attention.

"Steady," he called as he lined up his shot.

The chauffeur kept the car going straight, hitting the accelerator as hard as he could. The car lunged forward a little but Thea grabbed onto James' jacket so that he didn't fall out.

He fired. Livingston's car seemed to slow down. He fired again and the black automobile swerved off of the road, plowing into the ditch and crashing into a fence.

Once they got closer, she saw that James had shot one of the tires. As the car rolled to the side of the road, James pushed the door open and jumped out. Thea waited until the automobile came to a complete stop before she followed him.

James walked forward, cocked the shotgun, and aimed it at Mr. Livingston as he pushed his door open. The man's movements were slow, like he was struggling. Blood dripped from a gash on his head from where he hit against the steering wheel.

"Keep your hands where I can see them," James ordered, keeping the gun trained on him. The other man looked up at him, his eyes widening. "No sudden movements. Move slowly."

Livingston held both hands up as he climbed out. His eyes raged with fury as he glared at her and James. He jerked towards the seat. Livingston fired a shot before Thea realized he held Leslie's revolver.

He didn't get a second shot.

James fired. The noise from the shotgun was deafening in comparison to the other. The revolver flew from Livingston's hand as he screamed. James cocked the gun again.

"Don't even think about it," her brother warned as Livingston eyed the revolver again.

Mr. Livingston swallowed and cradled his injured hand.

"Walk towards me." James didn't take his eyes off of the other man. "You didn't happen to bring anything to tie him up with, did you?"

Thea shook her head.

"You can't do this!" the man growled. "I didn't do anything!"

Thea crossed her arms. "Is that why you attacked Inspector Thayne or tried to kill your wife? Or why you murdered your brother and Kate?"

Livingston snarled, his eyes feral. "I didn't kill my brother!"

The vehemence with which he spat those words was overwhelming. His protests fell on deaf ears as another black car pulled up. Thea couldn't help but wonder why he would deny only one of the murders. By declaring he was innocent of one crime, he was admitting to the others.

And, she thought, *if he didn't do it, who did?*

Constable Mitchell and Inspector Anderson climbed out of the car.

"I thought I asked you not to get involved," Anderson called out, looking at Thea.

She shrugged, unrepentant.

"What brings you here, Inspector?" James asked. He didn't take his eyes off of Livingston.

Anderson ignored him, approaching Livingston. Constable Mitchell followed.

"I didn't kill my brother," Livingston told Anderson again as the inspector pulled out his handcuffs.

"You told your wife that you did."

Livingston's face turned purple as he sputtered.

"You should pull up his shirt." Four sets of eyes bulged as they stared at Thea. Livingston silenced. "Just to his ribs."

Constable Mitchell reached out and pulled Livingston's shirt up. A bloodied homemade bandage wrapped around his lower torso.

"Huh," the policeman muttered as he stared at it. "If you don't mind me asking, Lady Theodora, how did you know that was there?"

"Mrs. Livingston said she stabbed him when he attacked her."

"I want a doctor!" Livingston demanded.

The constable's eyes narrowed. "We'll get you one." Constable Mitchell looked at them. His gaze settled on James. "We have it from here."

James lowered the gun. "Of course."

"Thank you for your help." Unlike Anderson, who hadn't stopped glaring, Constable Mitchell sounded genuine. The two of them led Mr. Livingston to the car and they drove away.

CHAPTER TWENTY-NINE

THEY RODE BACK TO THE CASTLE IN NEAR SILENCE. EVERYTHING about Mr. Livingston's confession bothered her in a way that she couldn't set aside. If Mr. Livingston didn't kill his brother, who killed Francis Livingston?

It seemed most likely that it was another guest who had shot him, unless someone hid in the woods, waiting for the opportune moment. Everyone knew he'd be out there. The younger Mr. Livingston blackmailed so many people. It didn't seem so unlikely that one of those people had a secret that they'd kill to protect.

She glanced at James. Again, she noticed, he had seemed so comfortable walking into an unknown situation. By his own admission, he too had received one of the letters. He said it had been nothing good, something that he didn't want to be public knowledge. On the train, he had shot Mrs. Fletcher without blinking. Not that long ago, he'd shot the elder Mr. Livingston. Neither of those were kill shots but that didn't mean he didn't have it in him.

"What?" James asked, noticing her eyes on him.

Thea blinked, heart pounding wildly in her chest. Did she honestly think that James was a cold-blooded killer?

The sleeve of James' jacket was turning red with his blood. It was a fortunate distraction from her previous train of thought. "You're bleeding."

He looked down.

"You were shot," she realized. "He shot you!"

James glanced at it. "I think it was just a graze." He prodded his arm gently and hissed in pain. He looked back at her and spoke through clenched teeth, "Yeah, just grazed."

He was lying. Again. Was anything he said the truth? Was he even really her brother?

From that point, she was able to pass her staring off as concern, even if her stomach felt like it was in worse tangles than the bottom of her embroidery bag.

"Thea!" Charlie cried as they climbed out of the car. They had to be a sight for sore eyes. Thea wanted to take a bath, to scrub her skin until it was raw. "You're back. Are you all right?"

"I'm fine. I didn't do much."

James nodded along with her statement, despite the fact that it too was a lie.

"Is Doctor Watterson still here?" Thea asked her cousin before she turned to James. "We should get your arm tended to."

James shook his head.

"It's fine. I don't need—" he cut off with a yelp as Thea pressed her thumb into the wound. He stared at her as if he was seeing her for the first time.

She raised her eyebrows at him, daring him to argue back.

"I'll go get the doctor." She patted his shoulder as she passed. James glowered.

Once the doctor found James and forced him into a room to examine him, Thea headed upstairs to get ready for dinner. Once in her room, she told Bridget to draw her a bath. She didn't want to feel so sick inside from the thought that she was so horribly naïve as to blindly trust what James said.

After she got out of the bath, Bridget guided her into her room.

"Dinner is in less than a half hour!" the maid complained. "I need more time!"

"You'll do amazing work as always," Thea told her. "And I don't think anyone will complain tonight if I'm a few minutes late."

Bridget pouted as she forced Thea into the last dress that Molly had sent. It was two pieces, an amethyst-colored slip and a delicately beaded sheer black overdress. Her necklace matched the slip exactly. Pins were woven into her hair in an elaborate updo and Thea's eyes blinked up at Bridget in the mirror.

"I know the last week has been hard for you—"

"My lady, I've appreciated all you've done to get closure for us. To get justice for my friend."

"Well, you could still take the rest of the night off. I'm sure I can manage on my own."

Bridget smiled indulgently, like one would at a small child who had just said something incredibly silly. "I'll be here when you're finished, my lady."

Thea fought a grin from crossing her face as she stood. She scratched Mercury's ears as he lay at the foot of the bed. He had been quiet that afternoon, more mellow than he had been since she found him. She hoped that was a good sign. It felt like a good sign.

She pulled her gloves on. For a short while, she had forgotten all of her doubts from earlier. But as she faced the door, they crashed against her like a wave and she had to close her eyes for a moment. Thea paused, looking back at Bridget before she spoke.

"Will you look in a guest's room for me?"

———

DINNER WAS A BOISTEROUS AFFAIR THAT NIGHT. EVERYONE WAS in high spirits now that the murders had been solved and Inspector Anderson wasn't there to watch over their every move.

Wilhelmina surprised everyone by coming downstairs. Anthony escorted her to her seat. After her ordeal, no one would have blamed her if she wanted to hide in her room.

She stood proud, despite walking with a slight limp, looking like the woman from the train instead of acting as she had when Livingston was around. She wore a vibrant dress of aquamarine-colored satin and white lace and there wasn't a trace of sadness in her face.

"You poor, brave woman," Mrs. Erskine said in her usual condescending tone as Wilhelmina settled in her seat. "What will you do now?"

Wilhelmina didn't rise to take the bait. "I think I'll return to London. I have some friends who I'd love to visit."

"That sounds lovely," Lady Thayne said softly, offering her a smile.

"I'm going to be in London next month," Charlie volunteered unnecessarily. "So is Thea. Perhaps we could meet at Harrods for tea."

Wilhelmina offered her a smile. "I think that sounds lovely."

Leslie sat down next to Thea. His eyes sparkled as he did so and she felt a thrill rush through her as he brushed his hand against hers.

"How are you doing?" she asked quietly.

"I got lucky. It could have been worse."

Across the table, James laughed with his cousin. He winced as his left arm knocked into the table. It lay uselessly in a sling beneath his jacket. The injury seemed to be worse than he tried to make it out to be.

He caught her staring and glanced away, refusing to meet her eyes.

"What happened to him?" Leslie asked, his breath against her ear.

"Livingston shot him. But he said it was just grazed."

The inspector flinched and refused to meet her eyes. Under the table, Thea reached for his hand and squeezed it until he looked at her.

"It's not your fault," she reassured him. "No one blames for you what happened."

"I shouldn't have let him get the upper hand over me. I knew what he was trying to do and I still let him escape with my weapon."

"Did you purposely let him escape?" Leslie shook his head. "Did you allow him to take your gun on purpose?" Another shake of his head. "Then it's not your fault. There was nothing you could have done."

He stared at her. "Thank you."

His fingers laced themselves between hers and they held onto each other through the meal as if they were the only thing keeping the other grounded.

Aunt Diana managed to turn the conversation to every-one's journeys the next day and Thea was thankful for that. The last thing they needed was to linger on all the unpleasant-ness of the last three days.

"Can we talk after dinner?" Leslie asked softly.

Thea nodded. She could feel the eyes of the others on them. She wondered if they could tell from how they were sitting that they were holding hands under the table.

"In the library," she answered back, keeping herself facing carefully ahead and not looking at him.

From her other side, Josiah looked at them, then at their hands intertwined between their chairs. He raised an eyebrow as she met his gaze. She looked away.

"Remember what I said," the Scotsman warned, his voice low enough that Leslie wouldn't hear over the noise of the conversation.

She tried not to give an indication that she had heard him. She didn't want Leslie to worry. In a way, it was kind of sweet how protective his brother was.

CHAPTER THIRTY

AFTER DINNER, THEA FOLLOWED THE OTHER LADIES BACK towards the drawing room. She stayed near the back, remaining in the hallway as they all went inside. Leslie waited for her by the fireplace in the library, his back to the door.

The room was warmer than the dining room but Thea found herself shivering. She wished she had a shawl to wrap around her. She closed the door behind her. She didn't want people to walk in or overhear something that they could misinterpret.

When he heard her at the door, he turned, a glass of amber colored liquor in his hand. "Would you like a drink?" She shook her head. "What happened this afternoon?"

"We caught up with Mr. Livingston. James had his shotgun and shot one of the tires on Livingston's automobile." The inspector nodded. "Then Livingston pulled your gun on us and fired."

"And then?" Leslie prodded.

"James shot Mr. Livingston." Thea frowned. "I'm beginning to see a pattern."

Leslie laughed but then her words seemed to click inside his head and he stared at her. "He shot him?"

"In the hand. Then Constable Mitchell and Inspector Anderson pulled up."

He nodded, staring at her, quiet and contemplative.

"What did my brother mean when he told you 'remember what I said?' at dinner?"

Thea flushed, glancing away so she wouldn't meet his eyes. "You heard that?"

"I was sitting right next to you. So?"

"He asked me to be careful not to hurt you."

Leslie stared for a moment before he shook his head, gripping the glass a little tighter. "He shouldn't have said anything to you. It wasn't his place."

Thea shook her head.

"I'm glad you're all right," Thea told Leslie, taking his hand again. He set his glass down on the mantle, raising his hand to run his thumb along her cheek and she looked down as she felt the blood rushing to her face. His hand dropped to her jaw, down to her chin, forcing her to look up.

"I'm glad you're all right too." He smiled. Her heart beat against her ribs. "And thank you for not running off by yourself this time."

He leaned forward, the two of them completely alone in the room. His lips pressed gently on her cheek.

A noise in the hallway sent them both to opposite ends of the fireplace, moments before Sylvia pushed the door open and walked inside.

"Oh," she said as she spotted them. She ran her eyes over them, and Thea hoped she didn't look nearly as awkward as she felt at the moment. "Am I interrupting something?"

"No," Leslie told her, his voice even.

"Well, then, let me join you."

"We were just leaving."

He offered Thea a hand. She took it and together they left the room.

Leslie escorted her to her bedroom. Her hand stayed in the crook of his arm the entire time as they walked upstairs.

Wilhelmina waited for Thea outside her bedroom door. Her face was flushed, though after everything that happened, it was hardly a wonder. The way she held herself seemed unstable and Thea was mostly surprised by the fact that she was still on her feet after everything.

"Hello," Thea said almost shyly.

"Mrs. Livingston," Leslie greeted, and Wilhelmina flinched.

"If you don't mind, I'd like to have a word alone with Thea."

"Of course." He turned. Her hand dropped from his arm. He took it in his hand, raised it to his lips, and kissed the back. "Good night, Thea. Good night, Mrs. Livingston. I hope you feel better in the morning."

Wilhelmina stood, eyes wide, watching them like she was watching a particularly interesting play. Leslie stepped back, letting Thea's hand fall as he walked away.

"What did I just interrupt?"

"Nothing," Thea lied, biting on her lip, still feeling a bit breathless.

Wilhelmina bumped Thea's arm playfully with her fan's ivory guards. "That was *not* nothing."

"He was just walking me to my room."

Wilhelmina crossed her arms, raising her eyebrows in surprise. "Do you mind if we go inside?"

Thea nodded and pushed the door open. Bridget was already inside. "Please give us a few minutes."

Bridget bowed her head. "Yes, my lady."

The maid disappeared from the room and Thea smiled at the other woman.

"How are you feeling?"

"I'm doing better."

Wilhelmina walked across the room, moving past the vanity, towards the desk where Mercury was sitting still, making him look more like an exotic sculpture than an actual cat.

"Who's this beauty?" she asked, holding out her hand. He leaned forward and sniffed at her knuckles. After a second, he seemed to deem her worthy of petting him and butted his head against her hand until she scratched behind his ears.

"That's Mercury. I found him in the tower."

Wilhelmina went stiff at the mention of the tower and she dropped her hand. Mercury let out a few meows of protest but Wilhelmina ignored him as she moved to the window and laid her head against the frame. Her shoulders drooped. She looked exhausted beyond belief from the past several days.

"Is he really gone?" The words were spoken so softly that Thea almost didn't hear them at first.

Thea nodded. "He's gone. Constable Mitchell took him."

Wilhelmina let out a breath.

"I can't believe he's gone," she choked out, relieved. "I just can't believe…"

She hid her face in her hands as she sobbed.

Thea crossed the room quickly, wrapping her arm around the woman's shoulders and rubbed her arm as comfortingly as she could. Wilhelmina collapsed into the chair.

"I feel like I've been under his thumb for so long. But now I'm free. I'm finally free," she repeated. She looked up at Thea, wiping her face with her fingers as she blindly searched for a handkerchief. "I don't want you to think I'm horribly cold…"

Her voice trailed off.

"I saw how he treated you. You deserve better than that. It's normal to be relieved that he's gone." She rubbed a hand on Wilhelmina's back. "It's going to be all right now. You'll see."

"Thank you so much, Thea, for everything," Wilhelmina said as she clung to her. Thea squeezed them back.

Once she had composed herself some, Wilhelmina stood up. She limped to the vanity to wipe her eyes in the mirror. She took a deep breath and glanced back at Thea.

"I'm sorry for that display. I know emotions sometimes make people uncomfortable."

Thea forced a smile on her face. "You've had a hard time. I think some emotion is natural. You should go get some rest now."

She still seemed embarrassed, her hands rubbing her arms. "Yes, I will. Good night."

"Sleep well."

Wilhelmina pulled the door open and walked out.

Exhausted, Thea sat down on the edge of her bed, resting her head against one of the bed posts as her eyelids grew heavy. Mercury jumped off the desk, padded over, and leaped onto the bed. He curled against her thigh and whined softly until Thea ran her hand along his back, even as her eyes drooped shut.

And that was how Bridget found them when she came back upstairs later.

CHAPTER THIRTY-ONE

"My lady?" a gentle voice asked, shaking her awake. Thea jerked away from the hand, her head and neck snapping as she did so. Mercury jumped up, meowing loudly in annoyance, before he stormed towards the head of the bed. She had a weird kink in her neck, where it hurt to move, and she had been having the best dream before she woke up. Not that she could remember it once she was awake. It was just a general feeling of happiness.

"I'm sorry to wake you," Bridget continued, her voice soft and the lights low, "but I need you to stand up for a couple of minutes while you change out of your gown."

Thea didn't want to. She wanted to sleep, even if the boning of her corset dug into her ribs because of the angle she was sitting.

"I'm sure that Mrs. Talbot won't be happy if you ruin her nice present."

Molly. Right. She had forgotten that in all of the excitement of the last couple days, she had rudely neglected to write back to Molly and thank her for the clothes.

"Bridget?" she muttered sleepily as the maid helped her

upright. "Would you remind me to write to Molly in the morning?"

"Of course, my lady."

Bridget helped her to the mirror and Thea collapsed onto the vanity stool. She was so tired, exhausted to the bone. The only thing she wanted to do was sleep tomorrow but she didn't want to miss everyone's departures. It would be the last chance she'd get to see them for a while, and she didn't want to miss out on it.

Her cheek still tingled from where Leslie had kissed her. She raised her hand to her face, tracing the spot with her fingertips as if she could still feel it. Thinking about it made the blood rush to her cheeks. Suddenly, she didn't feel so tired.

"My lady?" Bridget questioned. "Are you all right?"

Thea glanced down, not wanting to meet the maid's eyes. She felt too hot. If she were to look into the mirror, her face would be flushed. "I'm fine."

She was better than fine.

She glanced up, looking behind her. Bridget pressed her lips together, clearly fighting back whatever she was going to say. Instead, she chose to undo the buttons on the back of Thea's dress and helped her into a nightgown.

"I looked in the room you asked. It wasn't easy to find anything," the maid said softly, producing a note from her apron, "I found this in the heel of his shoe."

Suddenly alert, Thea took it between shaking fingers.

"What made you look in the heel of a shoe?" Although, perhaps it wasn't so odd that she looked there considering everything else Bridget had done. "Never mind."

To His Majesty's Spy:
I'm sure my friends in Germany would be very interested in you.
The next time you go abroad, your reception might not be so
friendly.

*If you would like to avoid this, deliver £1,000 exactly at 9:30
pm tomorrow by the angel statue in the garden. Come alone.*

The letter was dated Saturday. A photograph was attached
to it. She recognized the street in Paris where it was taken and
the subject of the photo.

James had a motive for him to kill Francis Livingston.

Thea closed her eyes, her chest tight. The right thing to do
would be to give the letter to Leslie. It also felt like that would
be the worst thing she could do.

"My lady?" Bridget asked.

"You're sure this was from his room?" She didn't want it to
be true. More than anything, she didn't want it all to have been
a lie.

"Yes, my lady."

Thea opened her eyes. "We'll never talk about this again. I
never saw this. You never saw this."

The maid frowned in confusion. "Saw what?"

Thea let out a breath and dropped the letter in the fire. As
it burned, she climbed into her bed and didn't even hear
Bridget leave the room before she fell asleep.

At breakfast the next morning, everyone was downstairs,
even the ladies. The dining table was filled to capacity. Thea
wondered if she would have to fight to get a plate from the
sideboard.

James was already surrounded by Charlie and Sylvia, both
girls hanging onto his every word as Thea approached them.
For a second, she could almost forget about the letter. But
despite her words to Bridget, she had seen it and the realization
had seared itself into her brain.

"Thea!" Charlie exclaimed, her eyes alight.

"Good morning," she greeted, glancing at James' arm. It was still hidden in the sling. All he could do was let it rest and hope it healed soon.

"Mr. Poyntz was telling me about Mr. Baird's monoplane!" Her cousin's face glowed with excitement. "He watched them test it."

Thea knew as much from reading the articles James had written but the way Charlie spoke of it, you would have thought he had told her all of the secrets of the universe.

"He's scheduled to make an actual flight later in the month," James informed them. "Lady Charlotte was kind enough to invite me back to Ravenholm after I leave there."

Thea smiled, even as her stomach twisted. "Don't be fooled by her," she teased. "She just wants to hear about the plane."

Charlie gave a long, suffering sigh. "It's true. I have to know all about it."

"You'll be the first I tell," he promised the girl. "After my editor, of course."

"Of course." But her cousin was practically glowing.

Thea wondered how different life would have been if James had been raised by their mother. Charlie and Anthony would have been his cousins too, not just hers. He would have been older than her and Cecil. Thea had always wondered what it would be like to have an older sibling, rather than just a brat of a brother who married her best friend.

Leslie joined them from across the room. He caught her eye and they both looked away quickly. She wondered if his cheeks flared the same way hers had.

There were two chairs next to each other at the table and Thea took one of them, hoping that Leslie would sit beside her for his last meal at Ravenholm. Instead, James shoved his way in-between them, standing in the inspector's way.

"You don't mind, do you?" He set his plate down at the spot next to Thea. "I'm afraid I'm rather tired of holding this."

James gave Leslie an innocent smile as he gripped the back of the chair with his good hand. The inspector rolled his eyes in return.

"Of course not." He managed to sound incredibly vexed by the fact that James wanted to sit there in just those three words but he didn't argue, taking an open spot across the table.

"Please be honest," James teased once he had sat down, clearly unaware of the irony of his words. "What happened between the two of you?"

"You're as bad as Wilhelmina."

He laughed. "If she's noticed after everything she's been through, then neither of you are being subtle."

Thea pushed her fork into a bite of her eggs. "There's nothing to be said."

"My dear Theodora, if I believed that, I would have never become a reporter in the first place."

She shot him a glare that he conveniently looked away for.

"I hate you," she muttered.

"No, you don't."

She stayed silent. She didn't hate him. She was grateful that he had been there with her the day before. Thea had no idea what she would have done if she had come across Mr. Livingston on her own. But she could never trust him. Her father always said, "Once a liar, always a liar."

"You could come with me to see the monoplane," he offered. "You and Charlotte both."

She bit her lip. "I'd say yes. I know Charlie would in a heartbeat…"

"But?" he prodded.

"I shouldn't just take her without Aunt Diana's permission."

He nodded. "That makes sense. Think about it though."

"I will."

She glanced at her cousin, watching the girl talk animatedly across the table.

"I'll see," she told him and watched as his face lit up. "It'd be nice to get away from all the death and murder and mysteries for a while."

"I thought you needed some excitement." She fought the urge to stick her tongue out at him. It would have been easy to do so but instead Thea set her fork down on her dish and turned to him.

She folded her fingers and pressed her thumbs together. "If something happens, I don't want to stand back."

James rolled his eyes.

"Just admit that you crave something more to life than being somebody's daughter or somebody's wife."

She kept her mouth shut. Even though it was true, she didn't want to validate him by admitting to it. James smirked.

"SIR," THEA OVERHEARD MR. SEMPLE SAY TO LESLIE AS THEY left the dining room, "Inspector Anderson is waiting for you in the library."

"Thank you for letting me know."

With that, he walked into the library and closed the door behind him. Inspector Anderson wouldn't appreciate her barging in to listen to the conversation. As soon as the others disappeared upstairs to pack, Thea moved down the hallway to the spot that Anthony had shown her and opened the door.

Once inside, she could hear Anderson's voice. The sound was a bit muffled, but it was far better than trying to listen through the main library doors.

"Livingston said that the maid stole some important papers and he confronted her. They argued, but he said she was still alive when he left her. He claims he doesn't know about any hidden compartment or how she got in there. But what I don't understand is why he went looking for her in the tower."

"I think this might explain it."

Through the shelves, Thea watched Leslie hand Anderson something that looked like papers. Were they the ones he had taken from her journal?

"Livingston knew about the compartment that the maid was found in," Leslie continued. "These were the papers the maid took. Lady Theodora found them in the maid's room. I'm sure if you compare his handwriting to these, it'll match."

"Then he was lying about not knowing about that space. He's probably lying about other things too."

Anderson was quiet for a moment. Thea wished he was facing the shelves so she could see his face. As long as she kept silent, they would never know that she was there.

"He also claims he didn't kill his brother. That's about the only thing I believe he didn't do. The slug that killed his brother was much smaller than the ones Mitchell and I got from the statue in the garden. The ones from the garden match his gun."

She watched Leslie tense.

"The one that killed his brother was the same size that half of the guests, including your mother, were using. It is entirely possible it was just a horrible hunting accident."

Thea closed her eyes, trying to keep from reacting. How could she ever be entirely sure if James was innocent?

CHAPTER THIRTY-TWO

THEA NEVER LIKED GOODBYES. IT FELT TOO MUCH LIKE THE end, a door closing never to be opened again. It was another reason she had avoided the hunts at Ravenholm for so long. Instead, she stayed out of sight, only saying farewell to the ones she actually cared about.

She brought Mercury downstairs in her jacket pocket. The kitten seemed to like riding there and enjoyed the attention the guests gave him. However, Thea had no sooner set her foot on the bottom step before Charlie appeared and commandeered him, saying that she wanted to play with him.

The Thaynes were among the first to leave, beaten only by the Erskines, who left immediately after breakfast. It seemed that the last few days were a bit much for them.

For now, as long as she stayed out of sight with Leslie, she could pretend that he wasn't leaving just yet. She liked spending time with him, even when they weren't trying to solve murders. She wished he could stay.

"I wonder if I might call on you in London?" he asked.

"I would like that very much."

"I look forward to seeing you again," he murmured, almost close enough that they could touch.

"Until next time."

His lips pressed against the bare skin of her palm and it took Thea a second to remember how to breathe again.

"Until then."

He started to walk away.

"Wait," she whispered, squeezing his hand tighter.

"What is it?" he asked as she led him inside the library. Nobody was in there, perhaps because most of the guests had already left.

"I don't want to say goodbye," she said, feeling a little foolish as she said so. She sounded like the heroine from one of Charlie's romance novels. Thea shook her head, looking down as she blushed.

Leslie's hand cradled her jaw, forcing her to look up at him.

"I don't want to either." He leaned in.

They could hear the people shuffling past in the hallway and he closed his eyes. A pained expression flashed across his face.

"Leslie?" Lady Thayne's voice called from outside the room.

He groaned and Thea let out a sigh of frustration.

"I should go," he muttered against her cheek.

"You should." She bit her lip. Her fingers tightened their hold on his jacket.

A male voice, Lord Thayne's perhaps, followed Lady Thayne's. "Wherever could that boy have gone?"

"I'll see you soon," Leslie promised. He slipped into the hallway and closed the door behind him.

"There you are!" Thea could hear his mother exclaim from outside. "I wondered where you had gotten off to."

Thea leaned her head against the wall and let out a breath.

She didn't think she could move. Even if she could, it would be safer to wait until everyone was outside before she joined the rest of her family in saying goodbye.

The hallway went quiet as the front door closed. Thea pushed herself up.

"I saw that," Wilhelmina's voice came from where she stood. Aunt Diana had decided that Wilhelmina should stay a few more days while she got her feet under her. Though from overhearing one of the whispered conversations between her aunt and uncle, Thea knew that they'd let Wilhelmina stay as long as she needed.

"Saw what?"

"Saw a certain inspector leave that room only a few moments before you came out." Wilhelmina cocked her head as she walked over to Thea. "Curious, isn't that?"

"Very. I'm just going to join my family."

Wilhelmina locked arms with Thea, laughing.

"You two are hardly discreet," she chided, her mood remarkably lighter than it had been at the start of the visit.

"It's really not like that," Thea protested, only to be met with an elegantly raised eyebrow.

"A room with a closed door, just the two of you…"

Thea blushed as they reached the front door to see the Thaynes off but she shook her head. "I'll tell you later."

"I'll hold you to that."

———

She found James tearing through his room when he should have been downstairs with his family. In truth, Thea wouldn't have even come up if Bridget hadn't seen him frantically searching when she came to clean his room. They both had a decent idea as to what he was looking for.

Still, Thea tried for a smile and hoped that it didn't look like a grimace.

"What's wrong?"

He shook his head but didn't look up as he searched through his briefcase. "I misplaced something."

"Do you want me to ask the maids to keep an eye out for it? she prodded. He lifted his head. As he walked towards her, a grin overtook his face. For a second, she thought he might reach out and ruffle her hair like she was a small child.

"I'm sure it'll turn up eventually." He shook his head. "I take it that my family's leaving?"

She nodded.

"Well, I'll see you when you come to the Isle of Bute." The grin fell from his face. "In the meantime, try to stay out of trouble."

"I make no promises."

"I know how hard you find it to avoid trouble."

She ducked her head as she laughed. He chuckled and she knew he wasn't being too serious.

"Farewell, little sister. I'll see you again soon."

He smirked at her as he passed through the door to join the rest of his family.

WHEN THEA WORKED UP THE NERVE TO GO DOWNSTAIRS, THE last of the cars was driving away. Charlie stood next to Wilhelmina and from the back, the similarities between them was striking.

"How was that for an adventure?" Thea asked Charlie as she approached. Her cousin let out an unhappy laugh and Mercury grumbled, whining until Thea took him and stroked his back. He settled down quickly then, purring loudly.

"I am never going in the tower again."

Wilhelmina's lips twitched at the corners.

"Besides," Charlie continued, glaring at both of them playfully, "when I said I wanted an adventure, I never meant murder."

"Then you shouldn't stay too close to Thea," Wilhelmina teased, bumping her shoulder into Thea's.

Thea barely resisted the urge to roll her eyes. It wasn't *her* fault that people kept getting murdered. She glanced between the two of them. "I promise not to go looking for dead people."

That kind of adventure would find her regardless of anything she did.

"THERE'S ONE THING I DON'T UNDERSTAND," THEA TOLD THE others as she piled some food onto her plate. "What happened to the treasure?"

Anthony's brow furrowed. Charlie frowned. "What treasure?"

"Are you talking about the Ravenholm treasure?" Great Aunt Mary asked.

Everyone turned towards the dowager countess.

"Mother? Do you know something?"

Great Aunt Mary smiled. "Of course, I do." She pointed to her necklace. The diamonds shone brightly. Each increased in size. The largest stone was in the center.

"That's from the treasure?" Wilhelmina rubbed against the spot on her head that had been hit.

"All that's left of it," the dowager countess confirmed.

Uncle Malcolm stared at his mother. "What do you mean all that's left of it?"

"Your father found it ages ago. We sold most of it off quietly."

Thea thought, *so much pain caused by a treasure that was long gone.*

On the way into the drawing room, Wilhelmina linked her arm with Thea's.

"It's always an adventure being around you. I look forward to more."

CHARACTERS

Thea's Family

Lady Theodora Prescott-Pryce – Thea lives with her widowed mother in London. Her brother, Cecil, the Earl, and his wife live at the Astermore Manor in Yorkshire. Thea travels aboard the *Flying Scotsman* annually to visit her cousins in Scotland during the fall.

Diana McNeil, Countess of Ravenholm, née Lady Diana Prescott-Pryce – Diana is Thea's paternal aunt. She married the Earl of Ravenholm and lives in Scotland.

Malcolm McNeil, 17th Earl of Ravenholm – Malcolm is Thea's uncle by marriage, Diana's husband, and the father of Anthony and Charlotte.

Anthony McNeil, Lord Auldkirk – Anthony is Thea's handsome older cousin.

Lady Charlotte "Charlie" McNeil – Charlie is Thea's fashion-obsessed younger cousin, who will be presented in court next Season.

Others (Also passengers on the *Flying Scotsman*)

Detective Inspector Leslie Thayne a.k.a. the Honorable Edward Leslie Thayne – Leslie is the younger son of a Scottish Baron and works in the Criminal Investigation Department of Scotland Yard.

Mrs. Wilhelmina Livingston – Wilhelmina is an American heiress married to The Hon. Ernest Livingston. She travelled to visit his friends in Scotland.

Mrs. Margaret Talbot a.k.a. Molly Forbes – Molly was Thea's maid and companion. After being framed for her husband Daniel Talbot's murder, she was cleared of the charges and now owns Fletcher's Department Store in London. She is pregnant.

James Poyntz – James is a journalist for the *West End Gazette* with a mysterious connection to Thea and her family.

ALSO SET IN THIS UNIVERSE:

Lady Thea's Mysteries

Book 1: Murder on the Flying Scotsman

ABOUT THE AUTHOR

Named for the famous fictional mystery writer Jessica Fletcher, Jessica Baker picked up a pen when she was in elementary school and never set it down.

Jessica lives in sunny Central Florida and is a member of the Florida Writers Association and National Sisters in Crime. When she's not writing, she freelances as a camera assistant in film which provides plenty of inspiration for her stories.

To learn more about Jessica and her books, visit her at www.jessicabakerauthor.com and for the latest information, subscribe to her newsletters.

Printed in Poland
by Amazon Fulfillment
Poland Sp. z o.o., Wrocław